The Fifth Mountain

THE FIFTH
MOUNTAIN

PAULO COELHO

TRANSLATED BY
CLIFFORD E. LANDERS

HarperPerennial
A Division of HarperCollinsPublishers

First HarperPerennial edition published 1999.

Designed by Jessica Shatan

The Library of Congress has catalogued the hardcover edition as follows:

Coelho, Paulo.
    [Monte cinco. English]
      The fifth mountain / Paulo Coelho ; translated from the Portuguese by Clifford E. Landers. — 1st ed.
      p. cm.
    ISBN 0-06-017544-3
    I. Landers, Clifford E.   II. Title.
PQ9698.13.0354613Q5613   1998
869.3—dc21   97-38387

ISBN 0-06-093013-6 (pbk.)

01 02 03 ❖/RRD 10 9 8

And he said, Verily I say unto you, No prophet is accepted in his own country.

But I tell you of a truth, many widows were in Israel in the days of Elias, when the heaven was shut up three years and six months, when great famine was throughout all the land;

But unto none of them was Elias sent, save unto Zarephath, a city of Sidon, unto a woman that was a widow.

Luke 4:24–26

NOTE FROM THE AUTHOR

◆ ◆ ◆

In my book *The Alchemist*, the central thesis lies in a phrase that King Melchizedek says to the shepherd boy Santiago: "When you want something, all the universe conspires in helping you to achieve it."

I believe this with all my heart. However, the act of living one's own destiny includes a series of stages that are far beyond our understanding, whose objective is always to take us back to the path of our Personal Legend—or to make us learn the lessons necessary to fulfill our own destiny. I think I can better illustrate what I am saying by relating an episode in my life.

On August 12, 1979, I went to sleep with a single certainty: at the age of thirty I was successfully making my way to the top of my career as a recording executive. I was working as artistic director for CBS in Brazil, and I had just been invited to the United

States to talk to the owners of the company, who would surely provide me with every opportunity to achieve all that I desired to do in my area. Of course my great dream—to be a writer—had been set aside, but what did that matter? After all, real life was very different from what I had imagined; there was no way to earn a living from literature in Brazil.

That night I made a decision: to abandon my dream. One had to adapt to circumstances and take advantage of opportunities. If my heart protested, I could deceive it by composing song lyrics whenever I wanted, and by doing some writing now and then for some newspaper. Besides, I was convinced that my life had taken a different path, but one no less exciting: a brilliant future awaited me in the world of the music multinationals.

When I woke up, I received a phone call from the president: I had just been fired, without further explanation. Although I knocked on various doors in the next two years, I never found a position again in that field.

When I finished writing *The Fifth Mountain*, I recalled that episode—and other manifestations of the unavoidable in my life. Whenever I thought myself the absolute master of a situation, something would happen to cast me down. I asked myself: why? Can it be that I'm condemned to always come close but never reach the finish line? Can God be so cruel that He would let me see the palm trees on the horizon only to have me die of thirst in the desert?

It took a long time to understand that it wasn't quite like

that. There are things that are brought into our lives to lead us back to the true path of our Personal Legend. Other things arise so we can apply all that we have learned. And, finally, some things come along to *teach* us.

In my book *The Pilgrimage*, I tried to show that these teachings need not be linked to pain and suffering; discipline and attentiveness alone are enough. Although this understanding has become an important blessing in my life, it still did not equip me to transit certain difficult moments that I experienced, even with total discipline and attentiveness.

One example is the case I have cited; I was a serious professional, made every effort to give the best there was in me, and had ideas that even today I consider worthwhile. But the unavoidable happened, at the very moment when I felt most secure and confident. I believe I am not alone in this experience; the unavoidable has touched the life of every human being on the face of the earth. Some have rebounded, others have given up— but all of us have felt the wings of tragedy brushing against us.

Why? To answer this question, I let Elijah lead me through the days and nights of Akbar.

PROLOGUE

◆ ◆ ◆

At the beginning of the year 870 B.C., a nation known as Phoenicia, which the Israelites called Lebanon, had marked almost three centuries of peace. Its inhabitants could take pride in their accomplishments; because they were not politically powerful, they had developed an enviable skill at negotiation as the only means of assuring survival in a world beset by constant war. An alliance made around the year 1000 B.C. with King Solomon of Israel had allowed the modernization of its merchant fleet and the expansion of trade. Since that time, Phoenicia had never stopped growing.

Its navigators had traveled to places as distant as Spain and the Atlantic Ocean, and there are theories—as yet unconfirmed—of their having left inscriptions in northeastern and southern Brazil. They carried glass, cedar, weapons, iron, and ivory. The inhabitants of the large cities such as Sidon, Tyre, and Byblos were familiar with numbers, astronomical calculations, the manufacture of wine, and for almost two hundred years had been using a set of characters for writing, which the Greeks knew as *alphabet*.

At the beginning of the year 870 B.C., a council of war was meeting in a distant place called Nineveh. A group of Assyrian generals had decided to send troops to conquer the nations located along the Mediterranean coast. Phoenicia had been selected as the first country to be invaded.

At the beginning of the year 870 B.C., two men hiding in a stable in Gilead, in Israel, expected to die in the next few hours.

PART I

"I HAVE SERVED A LORD WHO NOW ABANDONS ME INTO the hands of my enemies," said Elijah.

"God is God," the Levite replied. "He did not tell Moses whether He was good or evil; He simply said: *I am*. He is everything that exists under the sun—the lightning bolt that destroys a house, and the hand of man that rebuilds it."

Talking was the only way to ward off fear; at any moment, soldiers would open the door to the stable where they were hiding, discover them both, and offer the only choice possible: worship Baal, the Phoenician god, or be executed. They were searching house by house, converting the prophets or executing them.

Perhaps the Levite would convert and escape death. But for Elijah there was no choice: everything was happening through his own fault, and Jezebel wanted his head under all circumstances.

"It was an angel of the Lord who obliged me to speak to King Ahab and warn him that it would not rain so long as Baal was worshiped in Israel," he said, almost in a plea for absolution for having heeded what the angel had told him. "But God acts slowly; when the drought begins to take hold, Princess Jezebel will already have destroyed all who remain loyal to the Lord."

The Levite said nothing. He was reflecting on whether he should convert to Baal or die in the name of the Lord.

"Who is God?" Elijah continued. "Is it He who holds the sword of the soldier, the sword that executes those who will not betray the faith of our patriarchs? Was it He who placed a foreign princess on our country's throne, so that all this misfortune could befall our generation? Does God kill the faithful, the innocent, those who follow the law of Moses?"

The Levite made his decision: he preferred to die. Then he began to laugh, for the idea of death frightened him no longer. He turned to the young prophet beside him and attempted to calm him. "Ask God, since you doubt His decisions," he said. "I have accepted my fate."

"The Lord cannot wish us to be massacred without mercy," insisted Elijah.

"God is all-powerful. If He limited Himself to doing only that which we call good, we could not call Him the Almighty; he would command only one part of the universe, and there would exist someone more powerful than He, watching and judging His acts. In that case, I would worship that more powerful someone."

"If He is all-powerful, why doesn't He spare the suffering of those who love Him? Why doesn't He save them, instead of giving might and glory to His enemies?"

"I don't know," said the Levite. "But a reason exists, and I hope to learn it soon."

"You have no answer to this question."

"No."

The two men fell silent. Elijah felt a cold sweat.

"You are terrified, but I have already accepted my fate," the Levite said. "I am going out, to bring an end to this agony. Each time I hear a scream out there, I suffer, imagining how it will be when my time comes. Since we've been locked in here, I have died a hundredfold, while I could have died just once. If I am to be beheaded, let it be as quickly as possible."

He was right. Elijah had heard the same screams, and he had suffered beyond his ability to withstand.

"I'm going with you. I weary of fighting for a few more hours of life."

He rose and opened the stable door, allowing the sun to enter and expose the two men hiding there.

◆

THE LEVITE took him by the arm, and they began to walk. If not for one then another scream, it would have seemed a normal day in a city like any other—a sun that barely tingled the skin, the breeze coming from a distant ocean to moderate the temperature, the dusty streets, the houses built of a mixture of clay and straw.

"Our souls are prisoners of the terror of death, and the day is beautiful," said the Levite. "Many times before, when I felt at peace with God and the world, the temperature was horrible, the desert wind filled my eyes with sand and did not permit me to see a hand's span before me. Not always does His plan agree with what we are or what we feel, but be assured that He has a reason for all of this."

"I admire your faith."

The Levite looked at the sky, as if reflecting briefly. Then he turned to Elijah. "Do not admire, and do not believe so much; it was a wager I made with myself. I wagered that God exists."

"You're a prophet," answered Elijah. "You too hear voices and know that there is a world beyond this world."

"It could be my imagination."

"You have seen God's signs," Elijah insisted, beginning to feel anxiety at his companion's words.

"It could be my imagination," was again the answer. "In actuality, the only concrete thing I have is my wager: I have told myself that everything comes from the Most High."

◆

THE STREET was deserted. Inside their houses, the people waited for Ahab's soldiers to complete the task that the foreign princess had demanded: executing the prophets of Israel. Elijah walked beside the Levite, feeling that behind each door and window was someone watching him—and blaming him for what had happened.

"I did not ask to be a prophet. Perhaps everything is merely the fruit of my own imagination," thought Elijah.

But, after what had occurred in the carpenter's shop, he knew it was not.

◆

SINCE CHILDHOOD, he had heard voices and spoken with angels. This was when he had been impelled by his father and mother to seek out a priest of Israel who, after asking many questions, identified Elijah as a *nabi*, a prophet, a "man of the spirit," one who "exalts himself with the word of God."

After speaking with him for many hours, the priest told his father and mother that whatever the boy might utter should be regarded as earnest.

When they left that place, his father and mother demanded that Elijah never tell anyone what he saw and heard; to be a prophet meant having ties to the government, and that was always dangerous.

In any case, Elijah had never heard anything that might interest priests or kings. He spoke only with his guardian angel and heard only advice about his own life; from time to time he had visions he could not understand—distant seas, mountains populated with strange beings, wheels with wings and eyes. As soon as the visions disappeared, he—obedient to his father and mother—made every effort to forget them as rapidly as possible.

For this reason, the voices and visions became more and more infrequent. His father and mother were pleased, and they did not raise the matter again. When he came of an age to sustain himself, they lent him money to open a small carpentry shop.

◆

NOW AND AGAIN, he would gaze respectfully upon the other prophets, who walked the streets of Gilead wearing their customary cloaks of skins and sashes of leather and saying that the Lord had singled them out to guide the Chosen People. Truly, such was not his destiny; never would he be capable of evoking a trance through dancing or self-flagellation, a common practice among those "exalted by the voice of God," because he was afraid of pain. Nor would he ever walk the streets of Gilead, proudly displaying the scars from injuries achieved during a state of ecstasy, for he was too shy.

Elijah considered himself a common man, one who dressed like the rest and who tortured only his soul, with the same fears and temptations of simple mortals. As his work in the carpentry shop went on, the voices ceased completely, for adults and workers have no time for such things. His father and mother were happy with their son, and life proceeded in harmony and peace.

The conversation with the priest, when he was still a child, came to be merely a remote memory. Elijah could not believe that Almighty God must talk with men to have His orders obeyed; what had happened in his childhood was only the fantasy of a boy with nothing to do. In Gilead, his native city, there were those thought by the inhabitants to be mad. They were unable to speak coherently and incapable of distinguishing the voice of the Lord from the delirium of insanity. They spent their lives in the streets, preaching the end of the world and living on the charity of others. Even so, none of the priests considered them "exalted by the voice of God."

Elijah concluded in the end that the priests would never be sure of what they were saying. The "exalted of God" were a consequence of a country uncertain of its way, where brother fought brother, where new governments appeared with regularity. Prophets and madmen were one and the same.

When he learned of his king's marriage to Jezebel, princess of Tyre, he had thought it of little significance. Other kings of Israel had done the same, and the result had been a lasting peace in the region and an ever more important trade with Lebanon. Elijah scarcely cared if the people of the neighboring country believed in gods that did not exist or dedicated themselves to strange religious practices such as worshiping animals and mountains; they were honest in their negotiations, and that was what mattered most.

Elijah went on buying the cedar they brought in and selling the products of his carpentry shop. Though they were somewhat haughty and liked to call themselves "Phoenicians" because of the different color of their skin, none of the merchants from Lebanon had ever tried to take advantage of the confusion that reigned in Israel. They paid a fair price for the merchandise and made no comment about the constant internal wars or the political problems facing the Israelites.

◆

3PAULO COELHO

AFTER ASCENDING to the throne, Jezebel had asked Ahab to replace the worship of the Lord with that of the gods of Lebanon.

That too had happened before. Elijah, though outraged at Ahab's compliance, continued to worship the God of Israel and to observe the laws of Moses. "It will pass," he thought. "Jezebel seduced Ahab, but she will not succeed in convincing the people."

But Jezebel was a woman unlike others; she believed that Baal had brought her into the world to convert peoples and nations. Astutely and patiently, she began rewarding those who deserted the Lord and accepted the new deities. Ahab ordered a temple built for Baal in Samaria and in it raised an altar. Pilgrimages began, and the worship of the gods of Lebanon spread to all parts.

"It will pass. It may take a generation, but it will pass," Elijah went on thinking.

◆

THEN SOMETHING he was not expecting took place. One afternoon, as he was finishing a table in his shop, everything around him grew dark and thousands of tiny lights began twinkling about him. His head began to ache as never before; he tried to sit but could not move a muscle.

It was not his imagination.

"I'm dying," he thought at that instant. "And now I'll discover where God sends us after death: to the heart of the firmament."

One of the lights shone more brightly, and suddenly, as if coming from everywhere at once:

12

"And the word of the Lord came unto him, saying: Tell Ahab, that as surely as the Lord God of Israel liveth, before whom thou standest, there shall not be dew nor rain these years, but according to My word."

The next moment, all returned to normal: the carpentry shop, the afternoon light, the voices of children playing in the street.

◆

ELIJAH DID NOT SLEEP that night. For the first time in many years, the sensations of his childhood came back to him; and it was not his guardian angel speaking but "something" larger and more powerful than he. He feared that if he failed to carry out the order he might be cursed in his trade.

By morning, he had decided to do as he had been asked. After all, he was only the messenger of something that did not concern him; once the task was done, the voices would not return to trouble him.

It was not difficult to arrange a meeting with King Ahab. Many generations before, with the ascension of King Samuel to the throne, the prophets had gained importance in commerce and in government. They could marry, have children, but they must always be at the Lord's disposal so that the rulers would never stray from the correct path. Tradition held that thanks to these "exalted of God" many battles had been won, and that Israel survived because its rulers, when they did stray from the path of righteousness, always had a prophet to lead them back to the way of the Lord.

Arriving at the palace, he told the king that a drought would assail the region until worship of the Phoenician gods was forsaken.

The sovereign gave little importance to his words, but Jezebel—who was at Ahab's side and listened attentively to what Elijah was saying—began to ask a series of questions about the message. Elijah told her of the vision, of the pain in his head, of the sensation that time had stopped as he listened to the angel. As he described what had happened, he was able to observe closely the princess of whom all were talking; she was one of the most beautiful women he had ever seen, with long, dark hair falling to the waist of a perfectly contoured body. Her green eyes, which shone in her dark face, remained fixed on Elijah's; he was unable to decipher what they meant, nor could he know the impact his words were causing.

He left convinced that he had carried out his mission and could go back to his work in the carpentry shop. On his way, he desired Jezebel, with all the ardor of his twenty-three years. And he asked God whether in the future he could find a woman from Lebanon, for they were beautiful with their dark skin and green eyes full of mystery.

◆

HE WORKED for the rest of the day and slept peacefully. The next morning he was awakened before dawn by the Levite; Jezebel had convinced the king that the prophets were a menace to the growth and expansion of Israel. Ahab's soldiers had orders to execute all who refused to abandon the sacred task that God had conferred upon them.

To Elijah alone, however, no right of choice had been given: he was to be killed.

He and the Levite spent two days hidden in the stable south of Gilead while 450 *nabi* were summarily executed. But most of the prophets, who roamed the streets flagellating themselves and preaching the end of the world for its corruption and lack of faith, had accepted conversion to the new religion.

◆

A SHARP SOUND, followed by a scream, broke into Elijah's thoughts. He turned in alarm to his companion.

"What was that?"

There was no answer; the Levite's body fell to the ground, an arrow piercing his chest.

Standing before him, a soldier fitted another arrow into his bow. Elijah looked about him: the street with doors and windows tightly shut, the sun shining in the heavens, a breeze coming from an ocean of which he had heard so much but had never seen. He thought of running, but he knew he would be overtaken before he reached the next corner.

"If I must die, let it not be from behind," he thought.

The soldier again raised his bow. To Elijah's surprise, he felt neither fear nor the instinct to survive, nor anything else; it was as if everything had been determined long ago, and the two of them—he and the soldier—were merely playing roles in a drama not of their own writing. He remembered his childhood, the mornings and afternoons in Gilead, the unfinished work he would leave in his carpentry shop. He thought of his mother and father, who had never desired their son to be a prophet. He thought of Jezebel's eyes and of King Ahab's smile.

He thought how stupid it was to die at twenty-three, without ever having known a woman's love.

The soldier's hand released the string, the arrow slashed through the air, hummed past his right ear to bury itself in the dusty ground behind him.

The soldier rearmed his bow and pointed it. But instead of firing, he fixed his eyes on Elijah's.

"I am the greatest archer in all King Ahab's armies," he said. "For seven years I have never erred a shot."

Elijah turned to the Levite's body.

"That arrow was meant for you." The soldier's bow was still taut, and his hands were trembling. "Elijah was the only prophet who must be killed; the others could choose the faith of Baal," he said.

"Then finish your task."

He was surprised at his own calmness. He had imagined death so often during the nights in the stable, and now he saw that he had suffered unnecessarily; in a few seconds all would be ended.

"I can't," said the soldier, his hands still trembling, the arrow changing directions at every instant. "Leave, get out of my presence, because I believe God deflected my arrow and will curse me if I kill you."

It was then, as he discovered that death could elude him, that the fear of death returned. There was still the possibility of seeing the ocean, of finding a wife, having children, and completing his work in the shop.

"Finish this here and now," he said. "At this moment I am calm. If you tarry, I will suffer over all that I am losing."

The soldier looked about him to make certain that no one had witnessed the scene. Then he lowered his bow, replaced the arrow in its quiver, and disappeared around the corner.

Elijah felt his legs begin to weaken; the terror had returned in all its intensity. He must flee at once, disappear from Gilead, never again have to meet face-to-face a soldier with a drawn bow and an arrow pointed at his heart. He had not chosen his destiny, nor had he sought out Ahab in order to boast to his neighbors that he could talk with the king. He was not responsible for the massacre of the prophets—nor even for, one afternoon, having seen time stop and the carpentry shop transformed into a dark hole filled with points of light.

Mimicking the soldier's gesture, he looked to all sides; the street was deserted. He thought of seeing if he could still save the Levite's life, but the terror quickly returned, and before anyone else could appear, Elijah fled.

HE WALKED FOR MANY HOURS, TAKING PATHS LONG
since unused, until he arrived at the bank of the rivulet of
Cherith. He felt shame at his cowardice but joy at being alive.

He drank a bit of water, sat, and only then realized the situation in which he found himself: the next day he would need to
feed himself, and food was nowhere to be found in the desert.

He remembered the carpentry shop, his long years of work,
and having been forced to leave it all behind. Some of his neighbors were friends, but he could not count on them; the story of
his flight must have already spread throughout the city, and he
was hated by all for having escaped while he sent true men of
faith to martyrdom.

Whatever he had done in the past now lay in ruins—merely
because he had elected to carry out the Lord's will. Tomorrow,

and in the days, weeks, and months to come, the traders from Lebanon would knock on his door and someone would tell them the owner had fled, leaving behind a trail of innocent prophets' deaths. Perhaps they would add that he had tried to destroy the gods that protected heaven and earth; the story would quickly cross Israel's borders, and he could forget forever marrying a woman as beautiful as those in Lebanon.

◆

"THERE ARE the ships."

Yes, there were the ships. Criminals, prisoners of war, fugitives were usually accepted as mariners because it was a profession more dangerous than the army. In war, a soldier always had a chance to escape with his life; but the seas were an unknown, populated by monsters, and when a tragedy occurred, none were left to tell the story.

There were the ships, but they were controlled by Phoenician merchants. Elijah was not a criminal, a prisoner, or a fugitive but someone who had dared raise his voice against the god Baal. When they found him out, he would be killed and cast into the sea, for mariners believed that Baal and his gods governed the storms.

He could not go toward the ocean. Nor could he make his way north, for there lay Lebanon. He could not go east, where certain tribes of Israel were engaged in a war that had already lasted two generations.

◆

HE RECALLED the feeling of calm he had experienced in the presence of the soldier; after all, what was death? Death was an instant, nothing more. Even if he felt pain, it must pass at once, and then the Lord of Hosts would receive him in His bosom.

He lay down on the ground and looked at the sky for a long time. Like the Levite, he tried to make his wager. It was not a wager about God's existence, for of that he had no doubt, but about the reason for his own life.

He saw the mountains, the earth that soon would be beset by a long drought, as the angel of the Lord had said, but for now still had the coolness of many generations of rain. He saw the rivulet of Cherith, whose waters in a short time would cease to flow. He took his leave of the world with fervor and respect, and asked the Lord to receive him when his time was come.

He thought about the reason for his existence, and obtained no answer.

He thought about where he should go, and discovered that he was surrounded.

The following day he would go back and hand himself over, even if his fear of death returned.

He tried to find joy in the knowledge that he would go on living for a few more hours. But it was futile; he had just discovered that, as in almost all the days of a life, man is powerless to make a decision.

ELIJAH AWOKE THE NEXT DAY AND AGAIN LOOKED AT the Cherith.

Tomorrow, or a year from now, it would be only a bed of fine sand and smooth stones. The old inhabitants still referred to the site as Cherith, and perhaps they would give directions to those passing through by saying: "Such a place is on the bank of the river that runs near here." The travelers would make their way there, see the round stones and the fine sand, and reflect to themselves: "Here in this land there was once a river." But the only thing that mattered about a river, its flow of water, would no longer be there to quench their thirst.

Souls too, like rivulets and plants, needed a different kind of rain: hope, faith, a reason to live. When this did not come to pass, everything in that soul died, even if the body went on living;

and the people could say: "Here in this body there was once a man."

It was not the time to think about that. Again he remembered the conversation with the Levite just before they left the stable: what was gained from dying many deaths, if one alone sufficed? All he had to do was wait for Jezebel's soldiers. They would come, beyond any doubt, for there were few places to flee from Gilead; wrongdoers always fled to the desert—where they were found dead within a few days—or to the Cherith, where they were quickly captured.

The soldiers would therefore come soon. And he would rejoice at their sight.

◆

HE DRANK a bit of the crystalline water that ran beside him. He cleansed his face, then sought out shade where he could await his pursuers. A man cannot fight his destiny—he had already tried, and he had lost.

Despite the priests' belief that he was a prophet, he had decided to work as a carpenter; but the Lord had led him back to his path.

He was not the only one to abandon the life that the Lord had written for every person on earth. He had once had a friend with an excellent voice, whose father and mother had been unwilling to have him become a singer because it was a profession that brought dishonor to the family. A girl with whom he had been friends as a child could have been a dancer without equal; she too had been forbidden by her family, for the king might summon her, and no one knew how long his reign would last. Moreover, the atmosphere in the palace was considered sinful and hostile, ending permanently any possibility of a good marriage.

"Man was born to betray his destiny." God placed only impossible tasks in human hearts.

"Why?"

Perhaps because custom must be maintained.

But that was not a good answer. "The inhabitants of Lebanon are more advanced than are we, because they did not follow the customs of the navigators. When everyone else was using the same kind of ship, they decided to build something different. Many lost their lives at sea, but their ships continued to improve, and today they dominate the world's commerce. They paid a high price to adapt, but it proved to be worth the cost."

Perhaps mankind betrayed its destiny because God was not closer. He had placed in people's hearts a dream of an era when everything was possible—and then gone on to busy Himself with other things. The world had transformed itself, life had become more difficult, but the Lord had never returned to change men's dreams.

God was distant. But if He still sent His angels to speak to His prophets, it was because there was still something left to be done here. What could the answer be?

"Perhaps because our fathers fell into error, and they fear we will repeat their mistakes. Or perhaps they never erred, and thus will not know how to help us if we have some problem."

He felt he was drawing near. The rivulet was flowing at his side, a few crows were circling in the sky, the plants clinging insistently to life in the sandy, sterile terrain. Had they listened to the words of their forebears, what would they have heard?

"Rivulet, seek a better place for your limpid waters to reflect the brightness of the sun, for the desert will one day dry you up," the god of waters would have said, if perchance one existed. "Crows, there is more food in the forests than among rocks and sand," the god of the birds would have said. "Plants, spread your seeds far from here, because the world is full of humid, fertile ground, and you will grow more beautiful," the god of flowers would have said.

But the Cherith, like the plants and the crows, one of which had perched nearby, had the courage to do what other rivers, or birds, or flowers thought impossible.

Elijah fixed his gaze on the crow.

"I'm learning," he told the bird. "Though the lesson is a futile one, for I am condemned to death."

"You have discovered how everything is simple," the crow seemed to reply. "Having courage is enough."

Elijah laughed, for he was putting words into the mouth of a bird. It was an amusing game, one he had learned with a woman who made bread, and he decided to continue. He would ask the questions and offer himself an answer, as if he were a true sage.

The crow, however, took flight. Elijah went on waiting for Jezebel's soldiers to arrive, for dying a single time sufficed.

The day went by without anything happening. Could they have forgotten that the principal enemy of the god Baal still lived? Jezebel must know where he was; why did she not pursue him?

"Because I saw her eyes, and she is a wise woman," he told himself. "If I were to die, I would live on as a martyr of the Lord. If I'm thought of as just a fugitive, I'll be merely a coward who had no faith in his own words."

Yes, that was the princess's strategy.

◆

SHORTLY BEFORE NIGHTFALL, a crow—could it be the same one?—perched on the bough where he had seen it that morning. In its beak was a small piece of meat that it accidentally dropped.

To Elijah, it was a miracle. He ran to the spot beneath the tree, picked up the chunk of meat, and ate it. He didn't know from where it had come, nor did he wish to know; what was important was his being able to satisfy a small part of his hunger.

Even with his sudden movement, the crow did not fly away.

"This crow knows I'm going to starve to death here," he thought. "He's feeding his prey so he can have a better feast later."

Even as Jezebel fed the faith of Baal with news of Elijah's flight.

The two of them, man and crow, contemplated each other. Elijah recalled the game he had played that morning.

"I would like to talk to you, crow. This morning, I had the thought that souls need food. If my soul has not yet perished of hunger, it has something still to say."

The bird remained immobile.

"And, if it has something to say, I must listen. Because I have no one else with whom to speak," continued Elijah.

In his imagination Elijah was transformed into the crow.

"What it is that God expects of you?" he asked himself, as if he were the crow.

"He expects me to be a prophet."

"This is what the priests said. But it may not be what God desires."

"Yes, it is what He wants. An angel appeared to me in my shop and asked me to speak with Ahab. The voices I heard as a child—"

"Everyone hears voices as a child," interrupted the crow.

"But not everyone sees an angel," Elijah said.

This time the crow did not reply. After an interval, the bird—or rather, his own soul, delirious from the sun and loneliness of the desert—broke the silence.

"Do you remember the woman who used to make bread?" he asked himself.

◆

ELIJAH REMEMBERED. She had come to ask him to make some trays. While Elijah was doing as she asked, he heard her say that her work was a way of expressing the presence of God.

"From the way you make the trays, I can see that you have the same feeling," she had continued. "Because you smile as you work."

The woman divided human beings into two groups: those who took joy in, and those who complained about, what they did. The latter affirmed that the curse cast upon Adam by God was the only truth: "*Cursed is the ground for thy sake; in sorrow shalt thou eat of it all the days of thy life.*" They took no pleasure in work and were annoyed on feast days, when they were obliged to rest. They used the Lord's words as an excuse for their futile lives, forgetting that He had also said to Moses: "*For the Lord shall greatly bless thee in the land which the Lord thy God giveth thee for an inheritance to possess it.*"

"Yes, I remember the woman. She was right; I did enjoy my work in the carpentry shop. She taught me to talk to things."

"If you had not worked as a carpenter, you would not have been able to place your soul outside yourself, to pretend that it is a crow talking, and to understand that you are better and wiser than you believe," came the reply. "Because it was in the carpentry shop that you discovered the sacred that is in all things."

"I always took pleasure in pretending to talk to the tables

and chairs I built; wasn't that enough? And when I spoke to them, I usually found thoughts that had never entered my head. The woman had told me that it was because I had put the greater part of my soul into the work, and it was this part that answered me.

"But when I was beginning to understand that I could serve God in this way, the angel appeared, and—well, you know the rest."

"The angel appeared because you were ready," replied the crow.

"I was a good carpenter."

"It was part of your apprenticeship. When a man journeys toward his destiny, often he is obliged to change paths. At other times, the forces around him are too powerful and he is compelled to lay aside his courage and yield. All this is part of the apprenticeship."

Elijah listened attentively to what his soul was saying.

"But no one can lose sight of what he desires. Even if there are moments when he believes the world and the others are stronger. The secret is this: do not surrender."

"I never thought of being a prophet," Elijah said.

"You did, but you were convinced that it was impossible. Or that it was dangerous. Or that it was unthinkable."

Elijah rose.

"Why do you tell me what I have no wish to hear?"

Startled at the movement, the bird fled.

◆

THE BIRD RETURNED the next morning. Instead of resuming the conversation, Elijah began to observe it, for the animal always managed to feed itself and always brought him the food that remained.

A mysterious friendship developed between the pair, and Elijah began to learn from the bird. Observing it, he saw that it managed to find food in the desert, and he discovered that he could survive for a few more days if he learned to do the same. When the crow's flight turned into a circle, Elijah knew there was prey at hand; he would run to the spot and try to catch it. At first, many of the small animals living there escaped, but he gradually acquired the skill and agility to capture them. He used branches as spears and dug traps, which he disguised with a fine layer of twigs and sand. When the quarry fell, Elijah would divide his food with the crow, then set aside part to use as bait.

But the solitude in which he found himself was terrible and oppressive, which is why he decided again to pretend he was conversing with the crow.

"Who are you?" asked the crow.

"I'm a man who has found peace," replied Elijah. "I can live in the desert, provide for myself, and contemplate the endless beauty of God's creation. I have discovered that there resides in me a soul better than ever I thought."

They continued hunting together for another moon. Then

one night when his soul was possessed by sorrow, he asked himself again, "Who are you?"

"I don't know."

◆

ANOTHER MOON DIED and was reborn in the sky. Elijah felt that his body was stronger, his mind more clear. Tonight he turned to the crow, who was perched on the same branch as always, and answered the question he had asked some days before.

"I am a prophet. I saw an angel as I worked, and I cannot doubt what I am capable of doing, even if the entire world should tell me the opposite. I brought about a massacre in my country by challenging the one closest to the king's heart. I'm in the desert, as before I was in a carpentry shop, because my soul told me that a man must go through various stages before he can fulfill his destiny."

"Yes, and now you know who you are," commented the crow.

That night, when Elijah returned from the hunt, he went to drink and found that the Cherith had dried up. But he was so weary that he decided to sleep.

In his dream, his guardian angel, whom he had not seen for a long time, came to him.

"The angel of the Lord hath spoken to thy soul," said the guardian angel. "And hath ordered:

"*Get thee hence, and turn thee eastward, and hide thyself by the brook Cherith, that is before Jordan.*

"*Thou shalt drink of the brook; and I have commanded the ravens to feed thee there.*"

"My soul has heard," said Elijah in the dream.

"Then awake, for the angel of the Lord biddeth me hence and is desirous of speaking to thee."

Elijah leapt up, startled. What had happened?

Although it was night, the place was filled with light, and the angel of the Lord appeared.

"What hath brought thee here?" asked the angel.

"You brought me here."

"No. Jezebel and her soldiers caused thee to flee. This must thou never forget, for thy mission is to avenge the Lord thy God."

"I am a prophet, because you are in my presence and I hear your voice," Elijah said. "I have changed paths several times, as do all men. But I am ready to go to Samaria and destroy Jezebel."

"Thou hast found thy way, but thou mayest not destroy until thou learnest to build anew. I order thee:

"*Arise, get thee to Zarephath, which belongeth to Sidon, and dwell there; behold, I have commanded a widow woman there to sustain thee.*"

The next morning, Elijah looked for the crow, to bid him farewell. The bird, for the first time since he had arrived at the bank of the Cherith, did not appear.

ELIJAH JOURNEYED FOR DAYS BEFORE ARRIVING IN THE valley where lay the city of Zarephath, which its inhabitants knew as Akbar. When he was at the end of his strength, he saw a woman, dressed in black, gathering wood. The vegetation in the valley was sparse, and she had to be content with small, dry twigs.

"Who are you?" he asked.

The woman looked at the foreigner, not really understanding what he was saying.

"Bring me water to drink," Elijah said. "Bring me also a piece of bread."

The woman put aside the wood but still said nothing.

"Do not be afraid," Elijah insisted. "I am alone, hungry and thirsty, and haven't the strength to harm anyone."

"You're not from here," she said finally. "By the way you speak, you must be from the kingdom of Israel. If you knew me better, you'd be aware that I have nothing."

"You are a widow; this the Lord has told me. And I have even less than you. If you do not give me food and drink now, I will die."

The woman was taken aback; how could this foreigner know of her life?

"A man should feel shame at asking sustenance from a woman," she said, recovering.

"Do as I ask, please," Elijah insisted, knowing that his strength was beginning to fail. "When I am better, I will work for you."

The woman laughed.

"Moments ago, you told me something true; I am a widow, who lost her husband on one of my country's ships. I have never seen the ocean but I know it is like the desert: it slays those who challenge it . . . "

And she continued. "But now you tell me something false. As surely as Baal lives at the top of the Fifth Mountain, I have no food; there is nothing but a handful of flour in a barrel and a bit of oil in a flagon."

Elijah saw the horizon changing direction and knew he was about to faint. Gathering the last of his strength, he implored one final time, "I don't know if you believe in dreams; I don't know even if I believe in them. But the Lord told me that I would arrive here, and that I would find you. He has done things that caused me to doubt His wisdom, but never His existence. And thus the God of Israel asked that I tell the woman I met in Zarephath:

"*The barrel of meal shall not waste, neither shall the cruse of oil fail, until the day the Lord sendeth rain upon the earth.*"

Without explaining how such a miracle could come about, Elijah fainted.

The woman stood gazing down at the man who lay at her feet. She knew that the God of Israel was a mere superstition; the Phoenician gods were more powerful, and they had made her country one of the most respected nations on earth. But she was happy; usually she had to ask others for alms, and now, as had not happened for a long time, a man needed her. This made her feel stronger, for it was manifest that there were those in worse circumstances than she.

"If someone asks a favor of me, it is because I still have some use on this earth," she reflected.

"I'll do as he asks, if only to relieve his suffering. I too have known hunger, and know its power to destroy the soul."

She went to her house and returned with a piece of bread and some water. She kneeled, placed the foreigner's head in her lap, and began to moisten his lips. Within a few minutes, he had regained his senses.

She held out the bread to him, and Elijah ate quietly, looking at the valley, the ravines, the mountains pointing silently heavenward. Elijah could see the reddish walls of the city of Zarephath dominating the passage through the valley.

"Give me lodging with you, for I am persecuted in my own country," Elijah said.

"What crime have you committed?" she asked.

"I'm a prophet of the Lord. Jezebel has ordered the death of all who refuse to worship the Phoenician gods."

"How old are you?"

"Twenty-three," Elijah replied.

She looked pityingly at the young man before her. He had long, dirty hair and a beard that was still sparse, as if he wished to appear older than his years. How could a poor fellow like this challenge the most powerful princess in the world?

"If you're Jezebel's enemy, you're my enemy too. She is a princess of Tyre, whose mission when she married your king was to convert your people to the true faith, or so say those who have met her."

She pointed toward one of the peaks that framed the valley.

"Our gods have lived on the Fifth Mountain for many generations, and they have kept peace in our country. But Israel lives in war and suffering. How can you go on believing in the One God? Give Jezebel time to carry out her work and you'll see that peace will reign in your cities too."

"I have heard the voice of the Lord," Elijah replied. "But your people have never climbed to the top of the Fifth Mountain to discover what exists there."

"Anyone who climbs the Fifth Mountain will die from the fire of the heavens. The gods don't like strangers."

She fell silent. She had remembered dreaming, the night before, of a very strong light. From the midst of that light came a voice saying: "Receive the stranger who comes seeking you."

"Give me lodging with you, for I have nowhere to sleep," Elijah insisted.

"I told you that I'm poor. I barely have enough for myself and my son."

"The Lord asked you to let me stay; He never abandons those He loves. Do what I ask of you. I will work for you. I'm a carpenter, I know how to work cedar; there will be no lack of something to do. This way, the Lord will use my hands to keep His promise: *The barrel of meal shall not waste, neither shall the cruse of oil fail, until the day the Lord sendeth rain upon the earth.*"

"Even if I wished to, I would have no way to pay you."

"There is no need. The Lord will provide."

Confused by the previous night's dream, and even with the knowledge that the stranger was an enemy of the princess of Tyre, the woman decided to obey.

ELIJAH'S PRESENCE WAS SOON NOTICED BY THE NEIGH-bors. People commented that the widow had taken a foreigner into her house, in disrespect of the memory of her husband—a hero who had died attempting to expand his country's trade routes.

When she heard the rumors, the widow explained that he was an Israelite prophet, weary from hunger and thirst. And word spread that an Israelite prophet in flight from Jezebel was hiding in the city. A delegation went to see the high priest.

"Bring the foreigner to my presence," he ordered.

And it was done. That afternoon, Elijah was led to the man who, together with the governor and the leader of the military, controlled all that took place in Akbar.

"What have you come here to do?" he asked. "Do you not know that you are our country's enemy?"

"For years I have had commerce with Lebanon, and I respect your people and their customs. I am here because I am persecuted in Israel."

"I know the reason," said the high priest. "Was it a woman who made you flee?"

"In all my life, that woman was the most beautiful creature I have ever met, though I stood before her for only a brief moment. But her heart is like stone, and behind those green eyes hides the enemy who wishes to destroy my country. I did not flee; I await only the right moment to return."

The high priest laughed.

"If you're waiting for the right moment to return, prepare yourself to remain in Akbar for the rest of your life. We are not at war with your country; all we desire is to see the spread of the true faith, by peaceful means, throughout the world. We have no wish to repeat the atrocities committed by your people when you installed yourselves in Canaan."

"Is killing prophets a peaceful means?"

"If you cut off a monster's head, it ceases to exist. A few may die, but religious wars will be averted forever. And, from what the traders tell me, it was a prophet named Elijah who started all this, then fled."

The high priest stared at him, before continuing.

"A man who looked much like you."

"It is I," Elijah replied.

"Excellent. Welcome to the city of Akbar; when we need

something from Jezebel, we will pay for it with your head—the most important currency we have. Till then, seek out employment and learn to fend for yourself, because here there is no place for prophets."

Elijah was preparing to depart, when the high priest told him, "It seems that a young woman from Sidon is more powerful than your One God. She succeeded in erecting an altar to Baal, before which the old priests now kneel."

"Everything will happen as was written by the Lord," replied the prophet. "There are moments when tribulations occur in our lives, and we cannot avoid them. But they are there for some reason."

"What reason?"

"That is a question we cannot answer before, or even during, the trials. Only when we have overcome them do we understand why they were there."

◆

AS SOON AS ELIJAH had departed, the high priest called the delegation of citizens who had sought him out that morning.

"Do not concern yourselves about this," said the high priest. "Custom mandates that we offer hospitality to foreigners. Besides that, here he is under our control and we can observe his steps. The best way to know and destroy an enemy is to pretend to become his friend. When the time comes, he will be handed over to Jezebel, and our city will receive gold and other recompense. By then, we shall have learned how to destroy his ideas; for now, we know only how to destroy his body."

Although Elijah was a worshiper of the One God and a potential enemy of the princess, the high priest demanded that the right of asylum be honored. Everyone knew of the ancient custom: if a city were to deny shelter to a traveler, the sons of its inhabitants would later face the same difficulty. Since the greater part of Akbar had descendants scattered among the country's gigantic merchant fleet, no one dared challenge the law of hospitality.

Furthermore, it cost nothing to await the day when the Jewish prophet's head would be exchanged for large amounts of gold.

That night, Elijah supped with the widow and her son. As the Israelite prophet was now a valuable commodity to be bargained for in the future, several traders sent provisions enough to feed the three of them for a week.

"It appears the God of Israel is keeping His word," said the widow. "Not since my husband died has my table been as full as today."

LITTLE BY LITTLE ELIJAH BECAME PART OF THE LIFE OF Zarephath and, like all its inhabitants, came to call it Akbar. He met the governor, the commander of the garrison, the high priest, and the master glassmakers, who were admired throughout the region. When asked his reason for being there, he would tell the truth: Jezebel was slaying all the prophets in Israel.

"You're a traitor to your country, and an enemy of Phoenicia," they said. "But we are a nation of traders and know that the more dangerous a man is, the higher the price on his head."

And so passed several months.

AT THE ENTRANCE TO THE VALLEY, A FEW ASSYRIAN patrols had encamped, apparently intending to remain. The small group of soldiers represented no threat. But even so, the commander asked the governor to take steps.

"They have done nothing to us," said the governor. "They must be on a mission of trade, in search of a better route for their products. If they decide to make use of our roads, they will pay taxes—and we shall become even richer. Why provoke them?"

To complicate matters further, the widow's son fell ill for no apparent reason. Neighbors attributed the fact to the presence of the foreigner in her house, and the widow asked Elijah to leave. But he did not leave—the Lord had not yet called. Rumors began to spread that the foreigner had brought with him the wrath of the gods of the Fifth Mountain.

It was possible to control the army and calm the population about the foreign patrols. But, with the illness of the widow's son, the governor began having difficulty easing the people's minds about Elijah.

◆

A DELEGATION of the inhabitants of Akbar went to speak with the governor.

"We can build the Israelite a house outside the walls," they said. "In that way we will not violate the law of hospitality but will still be protected from divine wrath. The gods are displeased with this man's presence."

"Leave him where he is," replied the governor. "I do not wish political problems with Israel."

"What?" the townspeople asked. "Jezebel is pursuing all the prophets who worship the One God, and would slay them."

"Our princess is a courageous woman, and faithful to the gods of the Fifth Mountain. But, however much power she may have now, she is not an Israelite. Tomorrow she may fall into disfavor, and we shall have to face the anger of our neighbors; if we demonstrate that we have treated one of their prophets well, they will be kind to us."

The delegation left unsatisfied, for the high priest had said that one day Elijah would be traded for gold and other rewards. Nevertheless, even if the governor were in error, they could do nothing. Custom said that the ruling family must be respected.

IN THE DISTANCE, IN THE MIDDLE OF THE VALLEY, THE tents of the Assyrian warriors began to multiply.

The commander was concerned, but he had the support of neither the governor nor the high priest. He attempted to keep his warriors constantly trained, though he knew that none of them—nor even their grandfathers—had experience in combat. War was a thing of the past for Akbar, and all the strategies he had learned had been superseded by the new techniques and new weapons that other countries used.

"Akbar has always negotiated its peace," said the governor. "It will not be this time that we are invaded. Let the other countries fight among themselves: we have a weapon much more powerful than theirs—money. When they have finished destroying one another, we shall enter their cities—and sell our products."

The governor succeeded in calming the population about the Assyrians. But rumors were rife that the Israelite had brought the curse of the gods to Akbar. Elijah was becoming an ever greater problem.

◆

ONE AFTERNOON, the boy's condition worsened severely; he could no longer stand, nor could he recognize those who came to visit him. Before the sun descended to the horizon, Elijah and the widow kneeled at the child's bedside.

"Almighty Lord, who led the soldier's arrow astray and who brought me here, make this child whole again. He has done nothing, he is innocent of my sins and the sins of his fathers; save him, O Lord."

The boy barely moved; his lips were white, and his eyes were rapidly losing their glow.

"Pray to your One God," the woman asked. "For only a mother can know when her son's soul is departing."

Elijah felt the desire to take her hand, to tell her she was not alone and that Almighty God would attend him. He was a prophet; he had accepted that truth on the banks of the Cherith, and now the angels were at his side.

"I have no more tears," she continued. "If He has no compassion, if He needs a life, then ask Him to take me, and leave my son to walk through the valley and the streets of Akbar."

Elijah did all in his power to concentrate on his prayer; but that mother's suffering was so intense that it seemed to engulf the room, penetrating the walls, the door, everywhere.

He touched the boy's body; his temperature was not as high as in earlier days, and that was a bad sign.

◆

THE HIGH PRIEST had come by the house that morning and, as he had done for two weeks, applied herbal poultices to the boy's face and chest. In the preceding days, the women of Akbar had brought recipes for remedies that had been handed down for generations and whose curative powers had been proved on numerous occasions. Every afternoon, they gathered at the foot of the Fifth Mountain and made sacrifices so the boy's soul would not leave his body.

Moved by what was happening in the city, an Egyptian trader who was passing through Akbar gave, without charge, an extremely dear red powder to be mixed with the boy's food. According to legend, the technique of manufacturing the powder had been granted to Egyptian doctors by the gods themselves.

Elijah had prayed unceasingly for all this time.

But nothing, nothing whatsoever, had availed.

◆

"I KNOW WHY they have allowed you to remain here," the woman said, her voice softer each time she spoke, for she had gone many days without sleep. "I know there is a price on your head, and that one day you will be handed over to Israel in exchange for gold. If you save my son, I swear by Baal and the gods of the Fifth Mountain that you will never be captured. I know escape routes that have been forgotten for generations, and I will teach you how to leave Akbar without being seen."

Elijah did not reply.

"Pray to your One God," the woman asked again. "If He saves my son, I swear I will renounce Baal and believe in Him. Explain to your Lord that I gave you shelter when you were in need; I did exactly as He had ordered."

Elijah prayed again, imploring with all his strength. At that instant, the boy stirred.

"I want to leave here," the boy said in a weak voice.

His mother's eyes shone with happiness; tears rolled down her cheeks.

"Come, my son. We'll go wherever you like, do whatever you wish."

Elijah tried to pick him up, but the boy pushed his hand away.

"I want to do it by myself," he said.

He rose slowly and began to walk toward the outer room. After a few steps, he dropped to the floor, as if felled by a bolt of lightning.

Elijah and the widow ran to him; the boy was dead.

For an instant, neither spoke. Suddenly, the woman began to scream with all her strength.

"Cursed be the gods, cursed be they who have taken away my son! Cursed be the man who brought such misfortune to my home! My only child!" she screamed. "Because I respected the will of heaven, because I was generous with a foreigner, my son is dead!"

The neighbors heard the widow's lamentations and saw her son laid out on the floor of the house. The woman was still screaming, her fists pounding against the chest of the Israelite prophet beside her; he seemed to have lost any ability to react and did nothing to defend himself. While the women tried to comfort the widow, the men immediately seized Elijah by the arms and took him to the governor.

"This man has repaid generosity with hatred. He put a spell on the widow's house and her son died. We are sheltering someone who is cursed by the gods."

The Israelite wept, asking himself, "O my Lord and God, even this widow, who has been so generous to me, hast Thou chosen to afflict? If Thou hast slain her son, it can only be because I am failing the mission that has been entrusted to me, and it is I who deserve to die."

That evening, the council of the city of Akbar was convened, under the direction of the high priest and the governor. Elijah was brought to judgment.

"You chose to return hatred for love. For that reason, I condemn you to death," said the governor.

◆

"EVEN THOUGH YOUR HEAD is worth a satchel of gold, we cannot invite the wrath of the gods of the Fifth Mountain," the high priest said. "For later not all the gold in the world will bring peace back to this city."

Elijah lowered his head. He deserved all the suffering he could bear, for the Lord had abandoned him.

"You shall climb the Fifth Mountain," said the high priest. "You shall ask forgiveness from the gods you have offended. They will cause fire to descend from the heavens to slay you. If they do not, it is because they desire justice to be carried out at our hands; we shall be waiting for you at the descent from the mountain, and in accordance with ritual you will be executed the next morning."

Elijah knew all too well about sacred executions: they tore the heart from the breast and cut off the head. According to ancient beliefs, a man without a heart could not enter paradise.

"Why hast Thou chosen me for this, Lord?" he cried out, knowing that the men about him knew nothing of the choice the Lord had made for him. "Dost Thou not see that I am incapable of carrying out what Thou hast demanded of me?"

He heard no reply.

SHOUTING INSULTS AND HURLING STONES, THE MEN and women of Akbar followed in procession the group of guards conducting the Israelite to the face of the Fifth Mountain. Only with great effort were the soldiers able to contain the crowd's fury. After walking for half an hour, they came to the foot of the sacred mountain.

The group stopped before the stone altars, where people were wont to leave their offerings and sacrifices, their petitions and prayers. They all knew the stories of giants who lived in the area, and they remembered some who had challenged the prohibition only to be claimed by the fire from heaven. Travelers passing through the valley at night swore they could hear the laughter of the gods and goddesses amusing themselves from above.

Even if no one was certain of all this, none dared challenge the gods.

"Let's go," said a soldier, prodding Elijah with the tip of his spear. "Whoever kills a child deserves the worst punishment there is."

◆

ELIJAH STEPPED ONTO the forbidden terrain and began to climb the slope. After walking for some time, until he could no longer hear the shouts of the people of Akbar, he sat on a rock and wept; since that day in the carpentry shop when he saw the darkness dotted with brilliant points of light, he had succeeded only in bringing misfortune to others.

The Lord had lost His voices in Israel, and the worship of Phoenician gods must now be stronger than before. His first night beside the Cherith, Elijah had thought that God had chosen him to be a martyr, as He had done with so many others.

Instead, the Lord had sent a crow—a portentous bird—which had fed him until the Cherith ran dry. Why a crow and not a dove, or an angel? Could it all be merely the delirium of a man trying to hide his fear, or whose head has been too long exposed to the sun? Elijah was no longer certain of anything: perhaps Evil had found its instrument, and he was that instrument. Why had God sent him to Akbar, instead of returning him to put an end to the princess who had inflicted such evil on his people?

He had felt like a coward but had done as ordered. He had struggled to adapt to that strange, gracious people and their

completely different way of life. Just when he thought he was fulfilling his destiny, the widow's son had died.

"Why me?"

◆

HE ROSE, walked a bit farther until he entered the mist covering the mountaintop. He could take advantage of the lack of visibility to flee from his persecutors, but what would it matter? He was weary of fleeing, and he knew that nowhere would he find his place in the world. Even if he succeeded in escaping now, he would bear the curse with him to another city, and other tragedies would come to pass. Wherever he went, he would take with him the shadow of those deaths. He preferred to have his heart ripped from his chest and his head cut off.

He sat down again, amid the fog. He had decided to wait a bit, so that those below would think he had climbed to the top of the mountain; then he would return to Akbar, surrendering to his captors.

"The fire of heaven." Many before had been killed by it, though Elijah doubted that it was sent by the Lord. On moonless nights its glow crossed the firmament, appearing suddenly and disappearing just as abruptly. Perhaps it burned. Perhaps it killed instantly, with no suffering.

◆

AS NIGHT FELL, the fog dissipated. He could see the valley below, the lights of Akbar, and the fires of the Assyrian encampment. He heard the barking of their dogs and the war chants of their soldiers.

"I am ready," he said to himself. "I accepted that I was a prophet, and did everything I did as best I could. But I failed, and now God needs someone else."

At that moment, a light descended upon him.

"The fire of heaven!"

The light, however, remained before him. And a voice said:

"I am an angel of the Lord."

Elijah kneeled and placed his face against the ground.

"I have seen you at other times, and have obeyed the angel of the Lord," replied Elijah, without raising his head. "And yet I have done nothing but sow misfortune wherever I go."

But the angel continued:

"When thou returnest to the city, ask three times for the boy to come back to life. The third time, the Lord will hearken unto thee."

"Why am I to do this?"

"For the grandeur of God."

"Even if it comes to pass, I have doubted myself. I am no longer worthy of my task," answered Elijah.

"Every man hath the right to doubt his task, and to forsake it from time to time; but what he must not do is forget it. Whoever doubteth not himself is unworthy—for in his unquestioning belief in his ability, he committeth the sin of pride. Blessed are they who go through moments of indecision."

"Moments ago, you saw I was not even sure you were an emissary of God."

"Go, and obey what I have said."

AFTER MUCH TIME HAD PASSED, ELIJAH DESCENDED THE mountain to the place of the altars of sacrifice. The guards were awaiting him, but the multitude had returned to Akbar.

"I am ready for death," he said. "I have asked forgiveness from the gods of the Fifth Mountain, and now they command that, before my soul abandons my body, I go to the house of the widow who took me in, and ask her to take pity on my soul."

The soldiers led him back, to the presence of the high priest, where they repeated what the Israelite had said.

"I shall do as you ask," the high priest told the prisoner. "Since you have sought the forgiveness of the gods, you should also seek it of the widow. So that you do not flee, you will go accompanied by four armed soldiers. But harbor no illusion that you will convince her to ask clemency; when morning comes, we shall execute you in the middle of the square."

The high priest wished to inquire what he had seen atop the mountain, but in the presence of the soldiers the answer might be awkward. He therefore decided to remain silent, but he approved of having Elijah ask for forgiveness in public; no one else could then doubt the power of the gods of the Fifth Mountain.

Elijah and the soldiers went to the poor, narrow street where he had dwelled for several months. The doors and windows of the widow's house were open so that, following custom, her son's soul could depart, to go to live with the gods. The body was in the center of the small room, with the entire neighborhood sitting in vigil.

When they noticed the presence of the Israelite, men and women alike were horrified.

"Out with him!" they screamed at the guards. "Isn't the evil he has caused enough? He is so perverse that the gods of the Fifth Mountain refused to dirty their hands with his blood!"

"Leave to us the task of killing him!" shouted a man. "We'll do it right now, without waiting for the ritual execution!"

Standing his ground against the shoves and blows, Elijah freed himself of the hands that grasped him and ran to the widow, who sat weeping in a corner.

"I can bring him back from the dead. Let me touch your son," he said. "For just an instant."

The widow did not even raise her head.

"Please," he insisted. "Even if it be the last thing you do for me in this life, give me the chance to try to repay your generosity."

Some men seized him to drag him away. But Elijah resisted, struggling with all his strength, imploring to be allowed to touch the dead child.

Although he was young and determined, he was finally pulled away to the door of the house. "Angel of the Lord, where are you?" he cried to the heavens.

At that moment, everyone stopped. The widow had risen and come toward him. Taking him by the hands, she led him to where the cadaver of her son lay, then removed the sheet that covered him.

"Behold the blood of my blood," she said. "May it descend upon the heads of your line if you do not achieve what you desire."

He drew near, to touch the boy.

"One moment," said the widow. "First, ask your God to fulfill my curse."

Elijah's heart was racing. But he believed what the angel had told him.

"May the blood of this boy descend upon the heads of my father and mother and upon my brothers, and upon the sons and daughters of my brothers, if I do not do that which I have said."

Then, despite all his doubts, his guilt, and his fears, "*He took him out of her bosom, and carried him up into a loft, where he abode, and laid him upon his own bed.*

"And he cried unto the Lord, and said, O Lord, my God, hast Thou also brought evil upon the widow with whom I sojourn, by slaying her son?

"And he stretched himself upon the child three times, and cried unto the Lord, and said, O Lord, my God, I pray Thee, let this child's soul come into him again."

For long moments nothing happened. Elijah saw himself back in Gilead, standing before the soldier with an arrow pointing at his heart, aware that oftentimes a man's fate has nothing to do with what he believes or fears. He felt calm and confident as he had that day, knowing that, whatever the outcome might be, there was a reason that all of this had come to pass. Atop the Fifth Mountain, the angel had called this reason the "grandeur of God"; he hoped one day to understand why the Creator needed His creatures to demonstrate this glory.

It was then that the boy opened his eyes.

"Where's my mother?" he asked.

"Downstairs, waiting for you," replied Elijah, smiling.

"I had a strange dream. I was traveling through a dark hole, at a speed faster than the swiftest horse in Akbar. I saw a man— I am sure he was my father, though I never knew him. Then I came to a beautiful place where I wanted to stay; but another man—one I don't know but who seemed very good and brave— asked me kindly to turn away from there. I wanted to go on, but you awoke me."

The boy seemed sad; the place he had almost entered must be lovely.

"Don't leave me alone, for you made me come back from a place where I knew I'd be protected."

"Let us go downstairs," Elijah said. "Your mother wants to see you."

The boy tried to rise, but he was too weak to walk. Elijah took him in his arms and descended the stairs.

The people downstairs appeared overwhelmed by profound terror.

"Why are all these people here?" the boy asked.

Before Elijah could respond, the widow took the boy in her arms and began kissing him, weeping.

"What did they do to you, Mother? Why are you so sad?"

"I'm not sad, my son," she answered, drying her tears. "Never in my life have I been so happy."

Saying this, the widow threw herself on her knees and said in a loud voice:

"By this act I know that you are a man of God! The truth of the Lord comes from your words!"

Elijah embraced her, asking her to rise.

"Let this man go!" she told the soldiers. "He has overcome the evil that had descended upon my house!"

The people gathered there could not believe what they saw. A young woman of twenty, who worked as a painter, kneeled beside the widow. One by one, others imitated her gesture, including the soldiers charged with taking Elijah into captivity.

"Rise," he told them, "and worship the Lord. I am merely one of His servants, perhaps the least prepared."

But they all remained on their knees, their heads bowed.

"You spoke with the gods of the Fifth Mountain," he heard a voice say. "And now you can do miracles."

"There are no gods there. I saw an angel of the Lord, who commanded me to do this."

"You were with Baal and his brothers," said another person.

Elijah opened a path, pushing aside the kneeling people, and went out into the street. His heart was still racing, as if he had erred and failed to carry out the task that the angel had taught him. "To what avail is it to restore the dead to life if none believe the source of such power?" The angel had asked him to call out the name of the Lord three times but had told him nothing about how to explain the miracle to the multitude in the room below. "Can it be, as with the prophets of old, that all I desired was to show my own vanity?" he wondered.

He heard the voice of his guardian angel, with whom he had spoken since childhood.

"Thou hast been today with an angel of the Lord."

"Yes," replied Elijah. "But the angels of the Lord do not converse with men; they only transmit the orders that come from God."

"Use thy power," said the guardian angel.

Elijah did not understand what was meant by that. "I have no power but that which comes from the Lord," he said.

"Nor hath anyone. But all have the power of the Lord, and use it not."

And the angel said moreover:

"From this day forward, and until the moment thou returnest to the land thou hast abandoned, no other miracle will be granted thee."

"And when will that be?"

"The Lord needeth thee to rebuild Israel," said the angel. "Thou wilt tread thy land when thou hast learned to rebuild."

And he said nothing more.

PART II

THE HIGH PRIEST SAID THE PRAYERS TO THE RISING sun and asked the god of the storm and the goddess of animals to have mercy on the foolish. He had been told, that morning, that Elijah had brought the widow's son back from the kingdom of the dead.

The city was both frightened and excited. Everyone believed the Israelite had received his powers from the gods of the Fifth Mountain, and now it would be much more difficult to be rid of him. "But the right moment will come," he told himself.

The gods would bring about an opportunity to do away with him. But divine wrath had another purpose, and the Assyrians' presence in the valley was a sign. Why were hundreds of years of peace about to end? He had the answer: the invention of Byblos. His country had developed a form of writing accessible to all, even to those who were unprepared to use it. Anyone could learn it in a short time, and that would mean the end of civilization.

The high priest knew that, of all the weapons of destruction that man could invent, the most terrible—and the most powerful—was the word. Daggers and spears left traces of blood; arrows could be seen at a distance. Poisons were detected in the end and avoided.

But the word managed to destroy without leaving clues. If the sacred rituals became widely known, many would be able to use them to attempt to change the Universe, and the gods would become confused. Till that moment, only the priestly caste knew the memory of the ancestors, which was transmitted orally, under oath that the information would be kept in secret. Or else years of study were needed to be able to decipher the characters that the Egyptians had spread throughout the world; thus only those who were highly trained—scribes and priests—could exchange written information.

Other peoples had their rudimentary forms of recording history, but these were so complicated that no one outside the regions where they were used would bother to learn them. The invention of Byblos, however, had one explosive aspect: it could be used in any country, independent of the language spoken. Even the Greeks, who generally rejected anything not born in their cities, had adopted the writing of Byblos as a common practice in their commercial transactions. As they were specialists in appropriating all that was novel, they had already baptized the invention of Byblos with a Greek name: *alphabet*.

Secrets guarded through centuries of civilization were at risk of being exposed to the light. Compared to this, Elijah's sacrilege in bringing someone back from the other bank of the river of death, as was the practice of the Egyptians, meant nothing.

"We are being punished because we are no longer able to safeguard that which is sacred," he thought. "The Assyrians are at our gates, they will cross the valley, and they will destroy the civilization of our ancestors."

And they would do away with writing. The high priest knew the enemy's presence was not mere happenstance.

It was the price to be paid. The gods had planned everything with great care so that none would perceive that they were responsible; they had placed in power a governor who was more concerned with trade than with the army, they had aroused the Assyrians' greed, had made rainfall ever more infrequent, and had brought an infidel to divide the city. Soon the final battle would be waged.

AKBAR WOULD GO ON EXISTING EVEN AFTER ALL THAT, but the threat from the characters of Byblos would be expunged from the face of the earth forever. The high priest carefully cleaned the stone that marked the spot where, many generations before, the foreign pilgrim had come upon the place appointed by heaven and had founded the city. "How beautiful it is," he thought. The stones were an image of the gods——hard, resistant, surviving under all conditions, and without the need to explain why they were there. The oral tradition held that the center of the world was marked by a stone, and in his childhood he had thought about searching out its location. He had nurtured the idea until this year. But when he saw the presence of the Assyrians in the depths of the valley, he understood he would never realize his dream.

"It's not important. It fell to my generation to be offered in sacrifice for having offended the gods. There are unavoidable things in the history of the world, and we must accept them."

He promised himself to obey the gods: he would make no attempt to forestall the war.

"Perhaps we have come to the end of days. There is no way around the crises that grow with each passing moment."

The high priest took up his staff and left the small temple; he had a meeting with the commander of Akbar's garrison.

◆

HE WAS NEARLY to the southern wall when he was approached by Elijah.

"The Lord has brought a boy back from the dead," the Israelite said. "The city believes in my power."

"The boy must not have been dead," replied the high priest. "It's happened before; the heart stops and then starts beating again. Today the entire city is talking about it; tomorrow, they will recall that the gods are close at hand and can hear what they say. Their mouths will fall silent once more. I must go; the Assyrians are preparing for battle."

"Hear what I have to say: after the miracle last night, I slept outside the walls because I needed a measure of calm. Then the same angel that I saw on the Fifth Mountain appeared to me again. And he told me: Akbar will be destroyed by the war."

"Cities cannot be destroyed," said the high priest. "They

will be rebuilt seventy times seven because the gods know where they have placed them, and they have need of them there."

◆

THE GOVERNOR APPROACHED, with a group of courtiers, and asked, "What are you saying?"

"That you should seek peace," Elijah repeated.

"If you are afraid, return to the place from which you came," the high priest replied coldly.

"Jezebel and her king are waiting for fugitive prophets, to slay them," said the governor. "But I should like you to tell me how you were able to climb the Fifth Mountain without being destroyed by the fire from heaven."

The high priest felt the need to interrupt that conversation. The governor was thinking about negotiating with the Assyrians and might want to use Elijah for his purposes.

"Do not listen to him," he said. "Yesterday, when he was brought into my presence to be judged, I saw him weep with fear."

"My tears were for the evil I felt I had caused you, for I fear but two things: the Lord, and myself. I did not flee from Israel, and I am ready to return as soon as the Lord permits. I will put an end to your beautiful princess, and the faith of Israel shall survive this threat too."

"One's heart must be very hard to resist the charms of Jezebel," the high priest said ironically. "However, even should that happen, we would send another woman even more beautiful, as we did long before Jezebel."

The high priest was telling the truth. Two hundred years before, a princess of Sidon had seduced the wisest of all Israel's rulers—King Solomon. She had bid him construct an altar to the goddess Astarte, and Solomon had obeyed. For that sacrilege, the Lord had raised up the neighboring armies and Solomon had nearly lost his throne.

"The same will happen with Ahab, Jezebel's husband," thought Elijah. The Lord would bring him to complete his task when the time came. But what did it avail him to try to convince these men who stood facing him? They were like those he had seen the night before, kneeling on the floor of the widow's house, praising the gods of the Fifth Mountain. Custom would never allow them to think in any other way.

◆

"A PITY that we must honor the law of hospitality," said the governor, apparently already having forgotten Elijah's words about peace. "If not for that, we could assist Jezebel in her labor of putting an end to the prophets."

"That is not the reason for sparing my life. You know that I am a valuable commodity, and you want to give Jezebel the pleasure of killing me with her own hands. However, since yesterday, the people attribute miraculous powers to me. They think I met the gods on the Fifth Mountain. For your part, it would not upset you to offend the gods, but you have no desire to vex the inhabitants of the city."

The governor and the high priest left Elijah talking to himself and walked toward the city walls. At that moment the high priest decided that he would kill the Israelite prophet at the first opportunity; what had till now been only merchandise had been transformed into a menace.

◆

WHEN HE SAW them walk away, Elijah lost hope; what could he do to serve the Lord? He then began to shout in the middle of the square, "People of Akbar! Last night, I climbed the Fifth Mountain and spoke with the gods who dwell there. When I returned, I was able to reclaim a boy from the kingdom of the dead!"

The people gathered about him; the story was already known throughout the city. The governor and the high priest stopped and retraced their steps to see what was happening. The Israelite prophet was saying that he had seen the gods of the Fifth Mountain worshiping a superior God.

"I'll have him slain," said the high priest.

"And the population will rise up against us," replied the governor, who had an interest in what the foreigner was saying. "It's better to wait for him to commit an error."

"Before I descended from the mountain," continued Elijah, "the gods charged me with helping the governor against the threat from the Assyrians! I know he is an honorable man and wishes to hear me; but there are those whose interests lie with war and will not allow me to come near him."

"The Israelite is a holy man," said an old man to the governor. "No one can climb the Fifth Mountain without being struck dead by the fire of heaven, but this man did so—and now he raises the dead."

"Sidon, Tyre, and all the cities of Phoenicia have a history of peace," said another old man. "We have been through other threats worse than this and overcome them."

Several sick and lame people began to approach, opening a path through the crowd, touching Elijah's garments and asking to be cured of their afflictions.

"Before advising the governor, heal the sick," said the high priest. "Then we shall believe the gods of the Fifth Mountain are with you."

Elijah recalled what the angel had said the night before: only those powers given to ordinary people would be permitted him.

"The sick are asking for help," insisted the high priest. "We are waiting."

"First we must attend to avoiding war. There will be more sick, and more infirm, if we fail."

The governor interrupted the conversation. "Elijah will come with us. He has been touched by divine inspiration."

Though he did not believe any gods existed on the Fifth Mountain, the governor had need of an ally to help him to convince the people that peace with the Assyrians was the only solution.

◆

AS THEY WALKED to their meeting with the commander, the high priest commented to Elijah, "You don't believe anything you just said."

"I believe that peace is the only way out. But I do not believe the top of the Fifth Mountain is inhabited by gods. I have been there."

"And what did you see?"

"An angel of the Lord. I had seen this angel before, in several places I have been," replied Elijah. "And there is but one God."

The high priest laughed.

"You mean that, in your opinion, the same god who sends the storm also made the wheat, even though they are completely different things?"

"Do you see the Fifth Mountain?" Elijah asked. "From whichever side you look, it appears different, though it is the same mountain. Thus it is with all of Creation: many faces of the same God."

◆

THEY CAME TO THE TOP of the wall, from which they could see the enemy encampment in the distance. In the desert valley, the white tents sprang into sight.

Some time earlier, when the sentinels had first noted the presence of the Assyrians at one end of the valley, spies had said that they were there on a mission of reconnaissance; the commander had suggested taking them prisoner and selling them as slaves. The governor had decided in favor of another strategy: doing nothing. He was gambling that by establishing good relations with them, he could open up a new market for the glass manufactured in Akbar. In addition, even if they were there to prepare for war, the Assyrians knew that small cities will always side with the victor. In this case, all the Assyrian generals desired was to pass through without resistance on their way to Sidon and Tyre, the cities that held the treasure and knowledge of his people.

The patrol had encamped at the entrance to the valley, and little by little reinforcements had arrived. The high priest claimed to know the reason: the city had a well, the only well in several days' travel in the desert. If the Assyrians planned to conquer Tyre or Sidon, they needed that water to supply their armies.

At the end of the first month, they could still be expelled. At the end of the second month, Akbar could still win easily and negotiate an honorable withdrawal of the Assyrian soldiers.

They waited for battle to break out, but there was no attack. At the end of the fifth month, they could still win the battle. "They're going to attack very soon, because they must be suffering from thirst," the governor told himself. He asked the commander to draw up defense strategies and to order his men into constant training to react to a surprise attack.

But he concentrated only on preparations for peace.

◆

HALF A YEAR HAD PASSED, and the Assyrian army had made
no move. Tension in Akbar, which had grown during the first
weeks of occupation, had now diminished almost entirely. People
went about their lives: farmers once again returned to their fields;
artisans made wine, glass, and soap; tradesmen continued to buy
and sell their merchandise. Everyone believed that, as Akbar had
not attacked the enemy, the crisis would soon be settled through
negotiations. Everyone knew the governor was chosen by the
gods and that he always made the wisest decision.

When Elijah arrived in the city, the governor had ordered
rumors spread of the curse the foreigner brought with him; in this way,
if the threat of war became insurmountable, he could blame the presence of the foreigner as the principal cause of the disaster. The inhabitants of Akbar would be convinced that with the death of the
Israelite the Universe would return to normal. The governor would
then explain that it was too late to demand that the Assyrians withdraw; he would order Elijah killed and explain to his people that
peace was the best solution. In his view, the merchants—who desired
peace—would force the others to agree to this idea.

During these months, he had fought the pressure from the
high priest and the commander demanding that he attack at
once. The gods of the Fifth Mountain had never abandoned
him; now, with the miracle of the resurrection last night, Elijah's
life was more important than his execution.

◆

"WHY IS THIS foreigner with you?" asked the commander.

"He has been enlightened by the gods," answered the governor. "And he will help us to find the best solution." He quickly changed the subject. "The number of tents appears to have increased today."

"And it will increase even more tomorrow," said the commander. "If we had attacked when they were nothing but a patrol, they probably wouldn't have returned."

"You're mistaken. Some of them would have escaped, and they would have returned to avenge themselves."

"When we delay the harvest, the fruit rots," insisted the commander. "But when we delay resolving problems, they continue to grow."

The governor explained that peace, the great pride of his people, had reigned in Phoenicia for almost three centuries. What would the generations yet unborn say if he were to interrupt this era of prosperity?

"Send an emissary to negotiate with them," said Elijah. "The best warrior is the one who succeeds in transforming an enemy into a friend."

"We don't know exactly what they want. We don't even know if they desire to conquer our city. How can we negotiate?"

"There are threatening signs. An army does not waste its time on military exercises far from its own country."

Each day saw the arrival of more soldiers, and the governor mused about the amount of water necessary for all those men. In a short time, the entire city would be defenseless before the enemy army.

"Can we attack now?" the high priest asked the commander.

"Yes, we can. We shall lose many men, but the city will be saved. But we must decide quickly."

"We must not do that, Governor. The gods of the Fifth Mountain told me that we still have time to find a pacific solution," Elijah said.

Even after hearing the conversation between the high priest and the Israelite, the governor feigned agreement. To him, it made little difference whether Sidon and Tyre were ruled by Phoenicians, by Canaanites, or by Assyrians; what mattered was that the city be able to go on trading its products.

"We must attack," insisted the high priest.

"One more day," said the governor. "It may be that things will resolve themselves."

He must decide forthwith the best way to face the Assyrian threat. He descended from the wall and headed for the palace, asking the Israelite to go with him.

On the way, he observed the people around him: the shepherds taking their flocks to the mountains; the farmers going to the fields, trying to wrest from the arid soil sustenance for themselves and their families. Soldiers were exercising with spears, and a few newly arrived merchants displayed their wares in the square. Incredibly, the Assyrians had not closed off the road that traversed the valley from end to end; tradesmen still moved about with their merchandise and paid the city its tax for transport.

"Now that they have amassed such a powerful force, why have they not closed the road?" Elijah asked.

"The Assyrian empire needs the products that arrive in the ports of Sidon and Tyre," replied the governor. "If the traders were threatened, they would interrupt the flow of supplies. The consequences would be more serious than a military defeat. There must be some way to avoid war."

"Yes," said Elijah. "If they want water, we can sell it to them."

The governor said nothing. But he understood that he could use the Israelite as a weapon against those who desired war; should the high priest persist with the idea of fighting the Assyrians, Elijah would be the only one who could face him. The governor suggested they take a walk together, to talk.

THE HIGH PRIEST REMAINED ATOP THE WALL, OBSERVING the enemy.

"What can the gods do to deter the invaders?" asked the commander.

"I have carried out sacrifices at the Fifth Mountain. I have asked them to send us a more courageous leader."

"We should act as Jezebel has done: put an end to the prophets. A simple Israelite, who yesterday was condemned to die, is today used by the governor to entice the people to peace."

The commander looked at the mountain.

"We can have Elijah assassinated. And use my warriors to remove the governor from his position."

"I shall order Elijah killed," replied the high priest. "As for the governor, we can do nothing: his ancestors have been in power for several generations. His grandfather was our chieftain, who handed power down to his son, who in turn handed it to him."

"Why does custom forbid our bringing to power someone more efficient?"

"Custom exists to maintain the world in order. If we meddle with it, the world itself will perish."

The high priest looked about him. The heavens and the earth, the mountains and the valley, everything fulfilling what had been written for it. Sometimes the ground shook; at other times—such as now—there were long periods without rain. But the stars continued undisturbed in their place, and the sun had not fallen onto the heads of men. All because, since the Flood, men had learned that it was impossible to change the order of Creation.

In the past, only the Fifth Mountain had existed. Men and gods had lived together, strolled through the gardens of paradise, talking and laughing with one another. But human beings had sinned, and the gods expelled them; having nowhere to send them, they created the earth surrounding the mountain, so they could cast them there, keep vigil over them, and ensure that they would forever remember that they abided on a plane far inferior to that of the dwellers of the Fifth Mountain.

The gods took care, however, to leave open a path of return; if humanity carefully followed the way, it would one day go back to the mountaintop. So that this idea would not be forgotten, they charged the priests and the rulers with keeping it alive in the minds of the people.

All peoples shared the same belief: if the families anointed by the gods were removed from power, the consequences would be grave. No one now remembered why these families had been chosen, but everyone knew they were related to the divine families. Akbar had existed for hundreds of years, and its affairs had always been administered by the ancestors of the present governor; it had been invaded many times, had been in the hands of oppressors and barbarians, but with the passing of time the invaders had left or been expelled. Afterward, the old order would be reestablished and the people would return to the life they had known before.

The priests' obligation was to preserve this order: the world had a destiny, and it was governed by laws. The era of attempting to fathom the gods was past; now was the time to respect them and do their will. They were capricious and easily vexed.

If not for the harvest rituals, the earth would bring forth no fruit. If certain sacrifices were neglected, the city would be infested with fatal diseases. If the god of weather were provoked anew, he could cause wheat and men to cease to grow.

"Behold the Fifth Mountain," the high priest told the commander. "From its peak, the gods rule over the valley and protect us. They have an eternal plan for Akbar. The foreigner will be killed, or return to his own land; the governor will one day be no more, and his son will be wiser than he. All that we experience today is fleeting."

"We have need of a new chieftain," said the commander. "If we continue in the hands of this governor, we shall be destroyed."

The high priest knew that this was what the gods desired, in order to put an end to the writing of Byblos. But he said nothing; he was pleased to have evidence once again that, unwittingly or not, the rulers always fulfilled the destiny of the Universe.

◆

WALKING THROUGH THE CITY with the governor, Elijah explained to him his plans for peace and was made his counselor. When they arrived at the square, more sick people approached, but he said that the gods of the Fifth Mountain had forbidden him to heal. At the end of the afternoon, he returned to the widow's house; the child was playing in the street, and Elijah gave thanks for having been the instrument of the Lord's miracle.

She was awaiting him for the evening meal. To his surprise, there was a bottle of wine on the table.

"People brought gifts to please you," she said. "And I want to ask your forgiveness for the injustice I did you."

"What injustice?" asked Elijah, surprised. "Don't you see that everything is part of God's design?"

The widow smiled, her eyes shone, and he saw for the first time that she was beautiful. She was at least ten years older than he, but at that moment he felt great tenderness for her. He was not accustomed to such sentiments, and he was filled with fear; he remembered Jezebel's eyes, and the wish he had made upon leaving Ahab's palace—to marry a woman from Lebanon.

"Though my life has been useless, at least I had my son. And his story will be remembered, because he returned from the kingdom of the dead," the woman said.

"Your life is not useless. I came to Akbar at the Lord's order, and you took me in. If someday your son's story is remembered, I am certain that yours will be also."

The woman filled two cups. They drank to the sun, which was setting, and to the stars of heaven.

"You have come from a distant country, following the signs of a God I did not know but who now has become my Lord. My son has also returned from a far-off land, and he will have a beautiful tale to tell his grandchildren. The priests will preserve and pass on his words to generations yet to come."

It was through the priests' memory that cities knew of their past, their conquests, the ancient gods, and the warriors who defended the land with their blood. Even though there were now new ways to record the past, the inhabitants of Akbar had confidence only in the memory of their priests: one could write anything he chose, but no one could remember things that never were.

"And what have I to tell?" the widow continued, filling the cup that Elijah had quickly drained. "I don't have the strength or the beauty of Jezebel. My life is like all the rest: a marriage arranged by my father and mother when I was a child, household tasks when I came of age, worship on holy days, my husband always busy with other things. When he was alive, we never spoke of anything important. He was preoccupied with his trade, I took care of the house, and that was how we spent the best of our years.

"After his death, nothing was left for me except poverty and raising my son. When he becomes a man, he will cross the seas and I shall no longer matter to anyone. I feel neither hate nor resentment, only a sense of my own uselessness."

Elijah refilled his cup. His heart was beginning to give signs of alarm; he was enjoying being at this woman's side. Love could be a more frightening experience than standing before Ahab's soldier with an arrow aimed at his heart; if the arrow had struck him, he would be dead—and the rest was up to God. But if love struck him, he alone would have to take responsibility for the consequences.

"I have so wished for love in my life," he thought. And yet, now that it was before him—and beyond doubt it was there; all he had to do was not run away from it—his sole thought was to forget it as quickly as possible.

His mind returned to the day he came to Akbar, after his exile on the Cherith. He was so weary and thirsty that he could remember nothing except the moment he recovered from fainting, and seeing her drip water onto his lips. His face was very close to hers, closer than he had ever been to any woman in his entire life. He had noticed that she had Jezebel's green eyes, but with a different glow, as if they could reflect the cedar trees, the ocean of which he had often dreamed but never known, and—how could it be?—her very soul.

"I should so like to tell her that," he thought. "But I don't know how. It's easier to speak of the love of God."

Elijah took another sip. She sensed that she had said something that displeased him, and she decided to change the subject.

"Did you climb the Fifth Mountain?" she asked.

He nodded.

She would have liked to ask what he had seen there in the heights and how he had escaped the fire of the heavens. But he seemed loath to discuss it.

"You are a prophet," she thought. "Read my heart."

Since the Israelite had come into her life, everything had changed. Even poverty was easier to bear, for that foreigner had awakened something she had never felt: love. When her son had fallen ill, she had fought the entire neighborhood so he could remain in her house.

She knew that to him the Lord was more important than anything that took place beneath the sky. She was aware that it was a dream impossible of fulfillment, for the man before her could go away at any moment, shed Jezebel's blood, and never return to tell of what had happened.

Even so, she would go on loving him, because for the first time in her life, she knew freedom. She could love him, even if he never knew; she did not need his permission to miss him, to think of him every moment of the day, to await him for the evening meal, and to worry about the plots that people could be weaving against the foreigner.

This was freedom: to feel what the heart desired, with no thought to the opinion of the rest. She had fought with her neighbors and her friends about the stranger's presence in her house; there was no need to fight against herself.

Elijah drank a bit of wine, excused himself, and went to his room. She went out, rejoiced at the sight of her son playing in front of the house, and decided to take a short walk.

She was free, for love liberates.

◆

ELIJAH STARED at the wall of his room for a long time. Finally, he decided to invoke his angel.

"My soul is in danger," he said.

The angel said nothing. Elijah was in doubt about continuing the conversation, but now it was too late: he could not call him forth for no reason.

"When I'm with that woman, I don't feel good."

"Just the opposite," answered the angel. "And that disturbs thee, because thou canst come to love her."

Elijah felt shame, for the angel knew his soul.

"Love is dangerous," he said.

"Very," replied the angel. "And so?"

He suddenly disappeared.

His angel had none of the doubts that tormented Elijah's soul. Yes, he knew what love was; he had seen the king of Israel abandon the Lord because Jezebel, a princess of Sidon, had conquered his heart. Tradition told that King Solomon had come close to losing his throne over a foreign woman. King David had sent one of his best friends to his death after falling in love with his friend's wife. Because of Delilah, Samson had been taken prisoner and had his eyes put out by the Philistines.

How could he not know what love was? History was filled with tragic examples. And even had he no knowledge of sacred Scripture, he had the example of his friends, and of the friends of friends, lost in long nights of waiting and suffering. If he'd had a wife in Israel, it would have been difficult for him to leave his city when the Lord commanded, and he would be dead now.

"I am waging combat in vain," he thought. "Love will win this battle, and I will love her all of my days. Lord, send me back to Israel so that I may never have to tell this woman what I feel. Because she does not love me and will say to me that her heart lies buried alongside the body of her heroic husband."

THE NEXT DAY, ELIJAH MET WITH THE COMMANDER AGAIN and learned that more tents had been erected.

"What is the present complement of warriors?" he asked.

"I give no information to an enemy of Jezebel."

"I am a counselor of the governor," replied Elijah. "He named me his assistant yesterday afternoon. You have been informed of this, and you owe me an answer."

The commander felt an urge to put an end to the foreigner's life.

"The Assyrians have two soldiers for each one of ours," he finally replied.

Elijah knew that, to succeed, the enemy needed a much larger force.

"We are approaching the ideal moment to begin peace nego-

tiations," he said. "They will understand that we are being generous and we shall achieve better conditions. Any general knows
that to conquer a city five invaders are needed for each defender."

"They'll have that number unless we attack now."

"Even with all their lines of supply, they will not have
enough water for so many men. And the moment to send our
envoys will have come."

"What moment is that?"

"We shall allow the number of Assyrian warriors to increase
a bit more. When the situation becomes unbearable, they will be
forced to attack. But, with the proportion of three or four to one
of ours, they know they will end in defeat. That is when our
envoys will offer peace, safe passage, and the sale of water. This is
the governor's plan."

The commander said nothing and allowed the foreigner to
leave. Even with Elijah dead, the governor could still insist on the
idea. He swore to himself that if the situation came to that point
he would kill the governor, then commit suicide, because he had
no desire to witness the fury of the gods.

Nevertheless, under no circumstance would he let his people
be betrayed by money.

◆

"TAKE ME BACK to the land of Israel, O Lord," cried Elijah
every afternoon, as he walked through the valley. "Let not my
heart continue imprisoned in Akbar."

Following a custom of the prophets he had known as a child, he began lashing himself with a whip whenever he thought of the widow. His back became raw flesh, and for two days he lay delirious with fever. When he awoke, the first thing he saw was the woman's face; she had tended to his wounds with ointment and olive oil. As he was too weak to descend the stairs, she brought food to his room.

◆

AS SOON AS HE WAS WELL, Elijah resumed walking through the valley.

"Take me back to the land of Israel, O Lord," he said. "My heart is trapped in Akbar, but my body can still continue the journey."

The angel appeared. It was not the angel of the Lord, whom he had seen on the mountain, but the one who watched over him, and to whose voice he was accustomed.

"The Lord heareth the prayers of those who ask to put aside hatred. But He is deaf to those who would flee from love."

◆

THE THREE OF THEM supped together every night. As the Lord had promised, meal had never been wanting in the barrel nor oil in the vessel.

They rarely spoke as they ate. One night, however, the boy asked, "What is a prophet?"

"Someone who goes on listening to the same voices he heard as a child. And still believes in them. In this way, he can know the angels' thoughts."

"Yes, I know what you are speaking of," said the boy. "I have friends no one else can see."

"Never forget them, even if adults call it foolishness. That way you will always know God's will."

"I'll see into the future, like the soothsayers of Babylon," said the boy.

"Prophets don't know the future. They only transmit the words that the Lord inspires in them at the present moment. That is why I am here, not knowing when I shall return to my own country; He will not tell me before it is necessary."

The woman's eyes became sad. Yes, one day he would depart.

◆

ELIJAH NO LONGER cried out to the Lord. He had decided that, when the moment arrived to leave Akbar, he would take the widow and her son. But he would say nothing until the time came.

Perhaps she would not want to leave. Perhaps she had not even divined his feelings for her, for he himself had been a long time in understanding them. If it should happen thus, it would be better; he could then dedicate himself wholly to the expulsion of Jezebel and the rebuilding of Israel. His mind would be too occupied to think about love.

"The Lord is my shepherd," he said, recalling an ancient

prayer of King David. "He restoreth my soul. He leadeth me beside still waters.

"And He will not let me forget the meaning of my life," he concluded in his own words.

◆

ONE AFTERNOON he returned home earlier than was his wont, to find the widow sitting in the doorway of the house.

"What are you doing?"

"I have nothing to do," she replied.

"Then learn something. At this moment, many people have stopped living. They do not become angry, nor cry out; they merely wait for time to pass. They did not accept the challenges of life, so life no longer challenges them. You are running that same risk; react, face life, but do not stop living."

"My life has begun to have meaning again," she said, casting her gaze downward. "Ever since you came here."

◆

FOR A FRACTION of a second, he felt he could open his heart to her. But he decided not to take the risk; she must surely be referring to something else.

"Start doing something," he said, changing the subject. "In that way, time will be an ally, not an enemy."

"But what can I learn?"

Elijah thought for a moment.

"The writing of Byblos. It will be useful if one day you have to travel."

The woman decided to dedicate herself body and spirit to that study. She had never thought of leaving Akbar, but from the way he spoke perhaps he was thinking of taking her with him.

Once more, she felt free. Once more, she awoke at morning and strode smiling through the streets of the city.

"ELIJAH STILL LIVES," THE COMMANDER TOLD THE HIGH priest two months later. "You have not succeeded in having him killed."

"In all of Akbar there is no man who will carry out that mission. The Israelite has comforted the sick, visited the imprisoned, fed the hungry. When anyone has a dispute to settle with his neighbor, he calls on him, and all accept his judgments, because they are just. The governor is using him to increase his own standing among the people, but no one sees this."

"The merchants have no wish for war. If the governor finds favor enough with the people to convince them that peace is better, we shall never be able to expel the Assyrians. Elijah must be killed immediately."

The high priest pointed to the Fifth Mountain, its peak cloud-covered as always.

"The gods will not allow their country to be humiliated by a foreign power. They will take action; something will come to pass, and we shall be able to grasp the opportunity."

"What kind of opportunity?"

"I do not know. But I shall remain vigilant for the signs. Do not provide any further truthful information about the Assyrian forces. When you are asked, say only that the proportion of the invading warriors is still four to one. And go on training your troops."

"Why should I do that? If they attain the proportion of five to one, we are lost."

"No. We shall be in a state of equality. When the battle begins, you will not be fighting an inferior enemy and therefore cannot be branded a coward who abuses the weak. Akbar's army will confront an adversary as powerful as itself, and it will win the battle—because its commander chose the right strategy."

Piqued by vanity, the commander accepted the proposal. And from that moment, he began to withhold information from the governor and from Elijah.

TWO MORE MONTHS PASSED, AND ONE MORNING THE
Assyrian army reached the proportion of five soldiers for each of
Akbar's defenders. They could attack at any moment.

For some time Elijah had suspected that the commander was
lying about the enemy forces, but this might yet turn to his
advantage: when the proportion reached the critical point, it
would be a simple matter to convince the populace that peace
was the only solution.

These were his thoughts as he headed toward the place in the
square where, once a week, he was wont to help the inhabitants
of the city to settle their disputes. In general, the issues were triv-
ial: quarrels between neighbors, old people reluctant to pay their
taxes, tradesmen who felt they had been cheated in their business
dealings.

The governor was there; it was his custom to appear now and again to see Elijah in action. The ill will the prophet had felt toward him had disappeared completely; he had discovered that he was a man of wisdom, concerned with solving problems before they arose—although he was not a spiritual man and greatly feared death. On several occasions he had conferred upon Elijah's decisions the force of law. At other times Elijah, having disagreed with a decision, had with the passage of time come to see that the governor was right.

Akbar was becoming a model of the modern Phoenician city. The governor had created a fairer system of taxation, had improved the streets of the city, and administered intelligently the profits from the imposts on merchandise. There was a time when Elijah had asked him to do away with the consumption of wine and beer, for most of the cases he was called upon to settle involved aggression by intoxicated persons. The governor had told him that a city could only be considered great if that type of thing took place. According to tradition, the gods were pleased when men enjoyed themselves after a day's work, and they protected drunkards.

In addition, the region enjoyed the reputation of producing one of the finest wines in the world, and foreigners would be suspicious if the inhabitants themselves did not consume the drink. Elijah respected the governor's decision, and he came to agree that happy people produce more.

"You need not put forth so much effort," the governor told

him before Elijah began his day's work. "A counselor helps the government with nothing more than his opinions."

"I miss my country and want to return. So long as I am involved in activity, I feel myself of use and forget that I am a foreigner," he replied.

"And better control my love for her," he thought to himself.

◆

THE POPULAR TRIBUNAL had come to attract an audience ever alert to what took place. The people were beginning to gather: some were the aged, no longer able to work in the fields, who came to applaud or jeer Elijah's decisions; others were directly involved in the matters to be discussed, either because they had been the victims or because they expected to profit from the outcome. There were also women and children who, lacking work, needed to fill their free time.

He began the morning's proceedings: the first case was that of a shepherd who had dreamed of a treasure buried near the pyramids of Egypt and needed money to journey there. Elijah had never been in Egypt, but he knew it was far away, and he said that he would be hard pressed to find the necessary means, but if the shepherd were to sell his sheep to pay for his dream, he would surely find what he sought.

Next came a woman who desired to learn the magical arts of Israel. Elijah said he was no teacher, merely a prophet.

As he was preparing to find an amicable solution to a case in which a farmer had cursed another man's wife, a soldier pushed his way through the crowd and addressed the governor.

"A patrol has captured a spy," the newcomer said, sweating profusely. "He's being brought here!"

A tremor ran through the crowd; it would be the first time they had witnessed a judgment of that kind.

"Death!" someone shouted. "Death to the enemy!"

Everyone present agreed, screaming. In the blink of an eye the news spread throughout the city, and the square was packed with people. The other cases were judged only with great difficulty, for at every instant someone would interrupt Elijah, asking that the foreigner be brought forth at once.

"I cannot judge such a case," he said. "It is a matter for the authorities of Akbar."

"For what reason have the Assyrians come here?" said one man. "Can they not see we have been at peace for many generations?"

"Why do they want our water?" shouted another. "Why are they threatening our city?"

For months none had dared speak in public about the presence of the enemy. Though all could see an ever-growing number of tents being erected on the horizon, though the merchants spoke of the need to begin negotiations for peace at once, the people of Akbar refused to believe that they were living under threat of invasion. Save for the quickly subdued incursion of some insignificant tribe, war existed only in the memory of priests. They spoke of a nation called Egypt, with horses and chariots of war and gods that looked like animals. But that had all happened long ago; Egypt was no longer a country of import, and the warriors, with their dark skin and strange language, had returned to their own land. Now the inhabitants of Sidon and Tyre dominated the seas and were spreading a new empire around the world, and though they were tried warriors, they had discovered a new way of fighting: trade.

"Why are they restless?" the governor asked Elijah.

"Because they sense that something has changed. We both know that, from this moment on, the Assyrians can attack at any time. Both you and I know that the commander has been lying about the number of the enemy's troops."

"But he wouldn't be mad enough to say that to anyone. He would be sowing panic."

"Every man can sense when he is in danger; he begins to react in strange ways, to have premonitions, to feel something in the air. And he tries to deceive himself, for he thinks himself incapable of confronting the situation. They have tried to deceive themselves till now; but there comes a moment when one must face the truth."

The high priest arrived.

"Let us go to the palace and convene the Council of Akbar. The commander is on his way."

"Do not do so," Elijah told the governor in a low voice. "They will force on you what you have no wish to do."

"We must go," insisted the high priest. "A spy has been captured, and urgent measures must be taken."

"Make the judgment in the midst of the people," murmured Elijah. "They will help you, for their desire is for peace, even as they ask for war."

"Bring the man here!" ordered the governor. The crowd shouted joyously; for the first time, they would witness a conclave of the Council.

"We cannot do that!" said the high priest. "It is a matter of great delicacy, one that requires calm in order to be resolved!"

A few jeers. Many protests.

"Bring him here," repeated the governor. "His judgment shall be in this square, amid the people. Together we have worked to transform Akbar into a prosperous city, and together we shall pass judgment on all that threatens us."

The decision was met with clapping of hands. A group of soldiers appeared dragging a blood-covered, half-naked man. He must have been severely beaten before being brought there.

All noise ceased. A heavy silence fell over the crowd; from another corner of the square could be heard the sound of pigs and children playing.

"Why have you done this to the prisoner?" shouted the governor.

"He resisted," answered one of the guards. "He claimed he wasn't a spy and said he had come here to talk to you."

The governor ordered that three chairs be brought from his

palace. His servants appeared, bearing the cloak of justice, which he always donned when a meeting of the Council of Akbar was convened.

◆

THE GOVERNOR and the high priest sat down. The third chair was reserved for the commander, who was yet to arrive.

"I solemnly declare in session the tribunal of the Council of Akbar. Let the elders draw near."

A group of old men approached, forming a semicircle around the chairs. This was the council of elders; in bygone times, their opinions were respected and obeyed. Today, however, the role of the group was merely ceremonial; they were present to accept whatever the ruler decided.

After a few formalities such as a prayer to the gods of the Fifth Mountain and the declaiming of the names of several ancient heroes, the governor addressed the prisoner.

"What is it you want?" he asked.

The man did not reply. He stared at him in a strange way, as if he were an equal.

"What is it you want?" the governor repeated.

The high priest touched his arm.

"We need an interpreter. He does not speak our language."

The order was given, and one of the guards left in search of a merchant who could serve as interpreter. Tradesmen never came to the sessions that Elijah held; they were constantly occupied with conducting their business and counting their profits.

While they waited, the high priest whispered, "They beat the prisoner because they are frightened. Allow me to carry out this judgment, and say nothing: panic makes everyone aggressive, and we must show authority, lest we lose control of the situation."

The governor did not answer. He too was frightened. He sought out Elijah with his eyes, but from where he sat could not see him.

A merchant arrived, forcibly brought by the guard. He complained that the tribunal was wasting his time and that he had many matters to resolve. But the high priest, looking sternly at him, bade him to be silent and to interpret the conversation.

"What do you want here?" the governor asked.

"I am no spy," the man replied. "I am a general of the army. I have come to speak with you."

The audience, completely silent till then, began to scream as soon as these words were translated. They called it a lie and demanded the immediate punishment of death.

The high priest asked for silence, then turned to the prisoner.

"About what do you wish to speak?"

"The governor has the reputation of being a wise man," said the Assyrian. "We have no desire to destroy this city: what interests us is Sidon and Tyre. But Akbar lies athwart the route, controlling this valley; if we are forced to fight, we shall lose time and men. I come to propose a treaty."

"The man speaks the truth," thought Elijah. He had noticed that he was surrounded by a group of soldiers who hid from view the spot where the governor was sitting. "He thinks as we do. The Lord has performed a miracle and will bring an end to this dangerous situation."

The high priest rose and shouted to the people, "Do you see? They want to destroy us without combat!"

"Go on," the governor told the prisoner.

The high priest, however, again intervened.

"Our governor is a good man who does not wish to shed a man's blood. But we are in a situation of war, and the prisoner before us is an enemy!"

"He's right!" shouted someone from the crowd.

Elijah realized his mistake. The high priest was playing on the crowd while the governor was merely trying to be just. He attempted to move closer, but he was shoved back. One of the soldiers held him by the arm.

"Stay here. After all, this was your idea."

He looked behind: it was the commander, and he was smiling.

"We must not listen to any proposal," the high priest continued, his passion flowing in his words and gestures. "If we show we are willing to negotiate, we shall also be showing that we are fearful. And the people of Akbar are courageous; they have the means to resist any invasion."

"This prisoner is a man seeking peace," said the governor, addressing the crowd.

Someone said, "Merchants seek peace. Priests desire peace. Governors administer peace. But an army wants only one thing: war!"

"Can't you see that we were able to face the religious threat from Israel without war?" bellowed the governor. "We sent neither armies nor navies, but Jezebel. Now they worship Baal, without our having to sacrifice even one man on the battlefield."

"They didn't send a beautiful woman, they sent their warriors!" shouted the high priest even more loudly.

The people were demanding the Assyrian's death. The governor took the high priest by the arm.

"Sit down," he said. "You go too far."

"The idea of public judgment was yours. Or rather it was the Israelite traitor's, who seems to command the acts of the ruler of Akbar."

"I shall settle accounts with him later. Now, we must discover what the Assyrian wants. For many generations, men tried to impose their will by force; they spoke of what they wanted but cared not what the people thought—and all those empires have been destroyed. Our people have grown because they learned how to listen; this is how we developed trade—by listening to what the other person desires and doing whatever was possible to satisfy him. The result is profit."

The high priest nodded.

"Your words seem wise, and that is the greatest danger of all. If you were speaking folly, it would be simple to prove you wrong. But what you have just said is leading us into a trap."

Those in the front row heard the argument. Until that moment, the governor had always sought out the Council's opinion, and Akbar had an excellent reputation. Sidon and Tyre had sent emissaries to see how the city was administered; its name had even reached the ears of the emperor, and with some small good fortune, the governor might end his days as a minister at the imperial court.

Today, his authority had been challenged publicly. If he did not make a decision, he would lose the respect of the people—and no longer be capable of making important decisions, for none would obey him.

"Continue," he told the prisoner, ignoring the high priest's furious gaze and demanding that the interpreter translate his question.

"I have come to propose an agreement," said the Assyrian. "Allow us to pass, and we shall march against Sidon and Tyre. When those cities have been overcome—as they surely will be, because a great many of their warriors are on ships, occupied with trade—we shall be generous with Akbar. And keep you as governor."

"Do you see?" asked the high priest, again rising to his feet. "They think our governor barters Akbar's honor for an office!"

The multitude began to roar in outrage. That half-naked,

wounded prisoner wanted to lay down rules! A defeated man was proposing the surrender of the city! Several people rushed forward to attack him; with much effort, the guards managed to keep control of the situation.

"Wait!" said the governor, trying to speak above the din. "We have before us a defenseless man, one who can arouse in us no fear. We know that our army is better prepared, that our warriors are braver. We need prove that to no one. Should we decide to fight, we will win the battle, but the losses will be enormous."

Elijah closed his eyes and prayed that the governor could convince his people.

"Our ancestors spoke to us of the Egyptian empire, but it is no more," he continued. "Now we are returning once again to the Golden Age. Our fathers and their fathers before them were able to live in peace; why should we be the ones to break this tradition? Modern warfare is carried out through commerce, not on the field of battle."

Little by little, the crowd fell silent. The governor was succeeding!

When the noise ceased, he turned to the Assyrian.

"What you are proposing is not enough. To cross our lands, you must also pay taxes, as do the merchants."

"Believe this, Governor: Akbar has no choice," replied the prisoner. "We have men enough to raze this city and kill its every inhabitant. You have long been at peace and have forgotten how to fight, while we have been conquering the world."

Murmurs began again in the crowd. Elijah thought, "He cannot betray indecisiveness now." But it was difficult to deal with the Assyrian prisoner, who even while captive imposed his conditions. Moment by moment, more people were arriving; Elijah noticed that the tradesmen, concerned about the unfolding of events, had deserted their places of work to join the audience. The judgment had taken on a dangerous significance; there was no longer any way to retreat from making a decision, whether for negotiation or for death.

◆

THE ONLOOKERS began to take sides; some defended peace while others demanded that Akbar resist. The governor whispered to the high priest, "This man has challenged me in public. But so have you."

The high priest turned to him. And, speaking so none could hear, told him to condemn the Assyrian to death immediately.

"I do not ask, I demand. It is I who keep you in power, and I can put an end to that whenever I wish, do you understand? I know sacrifices to appease the wrath of the gods, if we are forced to replace the ruling family. It will not be the first time; even in Egypt, an empire that lasted thousands of years, there have been many cases of dynasties being replaced. Yet the Universe continued in its order, and the heavens did not fall upon our heads."

The governor turned pale.

"The commander is in the middle of the crowd, with some of his soldiers. If you insist on negotiating with this man, I will tell everyone that the gods have abandoned you. And you will be deposed. Let us go on with the judgment. And you shall do exactly as I order."

If Elijah had been in sight, the governor would have had a way out: he could have asked the Israelite prophet to say he had seen an angel on the Fifth Mountain, as he had recounted. He would recall the story of the resurrection of the widow's son. And it would be the word of Elijah—who had already proved himself able to perform a miracle—against the word of a man who had never demonstrated any type of supernatural power.

But Elijah had deserted him, and he had no choice. In any case, it was only a prisoner, and no army in the world starts a war because it lost one soldier.

"You win, for now," he told the high priest. One day he would negotiate something in return.

The high priest nodded. The verdict was delivered at once.

"No one challenges Akbar," said the governor. "And no one enters our city without permission from its people. You have attempted to do so, and are condemned to death."

From where he stood, Elijah lowered his eyes. The commander smiled.

THE PRISONER, FOLLOWED BY AN EVER LARGER THRONG, was led to a place beside the walls. There his remaining clothing was torn away, leaving him naked. One of the soldiers shoved him toward the bottom of a hollow located nearby. The people gathered around the hole, jostling against one another for a better view.

"A soldier wears his uniform with pride, and makes himself visible to the enemy, because he has courage. A spy dresses as a woman, because he's a coward," shouted the governor, for all to hear. "Therefore I condemn you to depart this life shorn of the dignity of the brave."

The crowd jeered at the prisoner and applauded the governor.

The prisoner said something, but the interpreter was no longer at hand, and no one understood him. Elijah succeeded in making his way through the crowd to the governor—but it was too late. When he touched his cloak, he was pushed away violently.

"The fault lies with you. You wanted a public judgment."

"The fault is yours," replied Elijah. "Even if the Council of Akbar had met in secret, the commander and the high priest would have imposed their will. I was surrounded by soldiers during the entire process. They had everything planned."

Custom decreed that it was the high priest's task to select the duration of the torture. He knelt, picked up a stone, and handed it to the governor; it was not large enough to grant a swift death, nor so small as to extend the suffering for long.

"First, you."

"I am being forced to do this," said the governor in a low voice so that only the high priest could hear. "But I know it is the wrong path."

"For all these years, you have forced me to take the harshest positions while you enjoyed the fruits of decisions that pleased the people," the high priest answered, also in a low voice. "I have had to face doubt and guilt, and endure sleepless nights, pursued by the ghosts of errors I may have made. But because I did not lose my courage, today Akbar is a city envied by the entire world."

People began looking for stones of the chosen size. For a time, the only sound was that of pebbles and stones striking one another. The high priest continued. "It is possible I am mistaken in condemning this man to death. But as to the honor of our city, I am certain we are not traitors."

◆

THE GOVERNOR raised his hand and threw the first stone; the prisoner dodged it. Immediately, however, the multitude, shouting and jeering, began to stone him.

The man attempted to protect his face with his arms, and the stones struck his chest, his back, his stomach. The governor wanted to leave; he had seen this many times before and knew that death was slow and painful, that the man's face would become a pulp of bones, hair, and blood, that the people would continue throwing stones even after life had left his body.

Within minutes, the prisoner would abandon his defense and lower his arms; if he had been a good man in this life, the gods would guide one of the stones to strike the front of his skull, bringing unconsciousness. If not, if he had committed cruelties, he would remain conscious until the final moment.

The multitude shouted, hurling stones with growing ferocity, and the condemned man tried to defend himself as best he could. Suddenly, however, he dropped his arms and spoke in a language that all could understand. Dismayed, the crowd interrupted the stoning.

"Long live Assyria!" he shouted. "At this moment I look upon the image of my people and die joyfully, because I die as a general who tried to save the lives of his warriors. I go to join the gods and am content because I know we shall conquer this land!"

"You see?" the high priest said. "He heard and understood everything that was said during the judgment!"

The governor agreed. The man spoke their language, and now he knew of the divisions in the Council of Akbar.

"I am not in hell, because the vision of my country gives me dignity and strength! The vision of my country brings me joy! Long live Assyria!" he shouted once more.

Recovered from its surprise, the crowd again began throwing stones. The man kept his arms at his sides, not attempting to resist; he was a brave warrior. A few seconds later, the mercy of the gods manifested itself: a stone struck his forehead and he fell unconscious to the ground.

"We can go now," the high priest said. "The people of Akbar will see to finishing the task."

◆

ELIJAH DID NOT GO back to the widow's house. He began walking through the desert, not knowing exactly where he wanted to go.

"The Lord did nothing," he said to the plants and rocks. "And He could have done something."

He regretted his decision and blamed himself for the death of yet another man. If he had accepted the idea of the Council of Akbar meeting in secret, the governor could have taken Elijah with him; then it would have been the two of them against the high priest and the commander. Their chances, though still small, would have been better than in the public judgment.

Worse yet, he had been impressed by the high priest's way of addressing the crowd; even though he disagreed with what he said, he was obliged to recognize that here was someone with a profound understanding of leadership. He would try to remember every detail of what he had seen, for one day, in Israel, he would have to face the king and the princess from Sidon.

He wandered aimlessly, looking at the mountains, the city, and the Assyrian encampment in the distance. He was a mere dot in this valley, and there was an immense world around him, a world so large that even if he traveled his entire life he would never find where it ended. His friends, and his enemies, might perhaps better understand the earth where they lived, might travel to distant countries, navigate unknown seas, love a woman without guilt. None of them still heard the angels of their childhood, nor offered themselves in the Lord's struggle. They lived out their lives in the present moment, and they were happy.

He too was a person like all the others, and in this moment walking through the valley he wished above all else never to have heard the voice of the Lord, or of His angels.

But life is made not of desires but of the acts of each person. He recalled that several times in the past he had tried to renounce his mission, but he was still there, in the middle of that valley, because this the Lord had demanded.

"I could have been a mere carpenter, O Lord, and still be useful to Thy work."

But there Elijah stood, carrying out what had been demanded of him, bearing within him the weight of the war to come, the massacre of the prophets by Jezebel, the death by stoning of the Assyrian general, his fear of loving a woman of Akbar. The Lord had given him a gift, and he did not know what to do with it.

In the middle of the valley, a light appeared. It was not his guardian angel, the one he heard but seldom saw. It was an angel of the Lord, come to console him.

"I can do nothing further here," said Elijah. "When will I return to Israel?"

"When thou learnest to rebuild," answered the angel. "But remember that which God taught Moses before a battle. Make use of every moment so that later thou wilt not regret, nor lament having lost thy youth. To every age in the life of a man, the Lord bestoweth upon him its own misgivings."

THE LORD SPOKE UNTO MOSES:

"Say unto them, Hear, O Israel, ye approach this day unto battle against your enemies: let not your hearts faint, fear not, and do not tremble, neither be ye terrified because of them. And what man is he that hath planted a vineyard, and hath not yet eaten of it? Let him also go and return unto his house, lest he die in the battle, and another man eat of it. And what man is there that hath betrothed a wife, and hath not taken her? Let him go and return unto his house, lest he die in the battle, and another man take her."

Elijah continued walking for some time, seeking to understand what he had heard. As he was readying to return to Akbar, he saw the woman he loved sitting on a rock facing the Fifth Mountain, a few minutes' walk from where he stood.

"What is she doing here? Does she know about the judgment, the death sentence, and the risks we have come to face?"

He must alert her at once. He decided to approach her.

She noticed his presence and waved. Elijah appeared to have forgotten the angel's words, for the feeling of uncertainty came rushing back. He tried to feign that he was worried about the problems of the city, so that she might not perceive the confusion in his heart and his mind.

"What are you doing here?" he asked when he drew close.

"I came in search of a bit of inspiration. The writing that

I'm learning made me think about the Designer of the valleys, of the mountains, of the city of Akbar. Some merchants gave me inks of every color, because they want me to write for them. I thought of using them to describe the world I live in, but I know how difficult that is: although I have the colors, only the Lord can mix them with such harmony."

She kept her gaze on the Fifth Mountain. She was a completely different person from the woman he had met some months before gathering wood at the city gate. Her solitary presence in the midst of the desert inspired confidence and respect in him.

"Why do all the mountains have names except the Fifth Mountain, which is known by a number?" asked Elijah.

"So as not to create conflict among the gods," she replied. "According to tradition, if men had given that mountain the name of a specific god, the others would have become furious and destroyed the earth. Therefore it's called the Fifth Mountain, because it's the fifth mountain we see beyond the walls. In this way, we offend no one, and the Universe continues in its place."

They said nothing for a time. The woman broke the silence.

"Besides reflecting on colors, I also think about the danger in the writing of Byblos. It might offend the gods of Phoenicia and the Lord our God."

"Only the Lord exists," interrupted Elijah. "And every civilized country has its writing."

"But it's different. When I was a child, I used to go to the square to watch the word painter who worked for the merchants. His drawings were based on Egyptian script and demanded skill and knowledge. Now, ancient and powerful Egypt is in decadence, without money to buy anything, and no one uses its language anymore; sailors from Sidon and Tyre are spreading the writing of Byblos to the entire world. The sacred words and ceremonies can be placed on clay tablets and transmitted from one people to another. What will become of the world if unscrupulous people begin using the rituals to interfere with the Universe?"

Elijah understood what the woman was saying. The writing of Byblos was based on a very simple system: the Egyptian drawings first had to be transformed into sounds, and then a letter was designated for each sound. By placing these letters in order, it was possible to create all possible sounds and to describe everything there was in the Universe.

Some of these sounds were very difficult to pronounce. That difficulty had been solved by the Greeks, who had added five more letters, called *vowels*, to the twenty-odd characters of Byblos. They baptized this innovation *alphabet*, a name now used to define the new form of writing.

This had greatly facilitated commercial contact among differing peoples. The Egyptian system had required much space and a great deal of ability to draw the ideas, as well as profound understanding to interpret them; it had been imposed on conquered nations but had not survived the decline of the empire. The system of Byblos, however, was spreading rapidly through the world, and it no longer depended on the economic might of Phoenicia for its adoption.

The method of Byblos, with the Greek adaptation, had pleased the traders of the various nations; as had been the case since ancient times, it was they who decided what should remain in history and what would disappear with the death of a given king or a given person. Everything indicated that the Phoenician invention was destined to become the common language of business, surviving its navigators, its kings, its seductive princesses, its wine makers, its master glassmakers.

"Will God disappear from words?" the woman asked.

"He will continue in them," Elijah replied. "But each person will be responsible before Him for whatever he writes."

She took from the sleeve of her garment a clay tablet with something written on it.

"What does that mean?" Elijah asked.

"It's the word *love*."

Elijah took the tablet in his hands, not daring to ask why she had given it to him. On that piece of clay, a few scratches summed up why the stars continued in the heavens and why men walked the earth.

He tried to return it to her, but she refused.

"I wrote it for you. I know your responsibility, I know that one day you will have to leave, and that you will become an enemy of my country because you wish to do away with Jezebel. On that day, it may come to pass that I shall be at your side, supporting you in your task. Or it may come to pass that I fight against you, for Jezebel's blood is the blood of my country; this word that you hold in your hands is filled with mystery. No one can know what it awakens in a woman's heart, not even prophets who speak with God."

"I know the word that you have written," said Elijah, storing the tablet in a fold of his cape. "I have struggled day and night against it, for, although I do not know what it awakens in a woman's heart, I know what it can do to a man. I have the courage to face the king of Israel, the princess of Sidon, the Council of Akbar, but that one word—*love*—inspires deep terror in me. Before you drew it on the tablet, your eyes had already seen it written in my heart."

They fell silent. Despite the Assyrian's death, the climate of tension in the city, the call from the Lord that could occur at any moment—none of this was as powerful as the word she had written.

Elijah held out his hand, and she took it. They remained thus until the sun hid itself behind the Fifth Mountain.

"Thank you," she said as they returned. "For a long time I had desired to spend the hours of sunset with you."

When they arrived home, an emissary from the governor was waiting for him. He asked Elijah to come with him immediately for a meeting.

◆

"YOU REPAID MY SUPPORT with cowardice," said the governor. "What should I do with your life?"

"I shall not live a second longer than the Lord desires," replied Elijah. "It is He who decides, not you."

The governor was surprised at Elijah's courage.

"I can have you decapitated at once. Or have you dragged through the streets of the city, saying that you brought a curse upon our people," he said. "And that would not be a decision of your One God."

"Whatever my fate, that is what will happen. But I want you to know I did not flee; the commander's soldiers kept me away. He wants war and will do everything to achieve it."

The governor decided to waste no more time on that pointless discussion. He had to explain his plan to the Israelite prophet.

"It's not the commander who wishes war; like a good military man he is aware that his army is smaller and inexperienced and that it will be decimated by the enemy. As a man of honor, he knows he risks causing shame to his descendants. But his heart has been turned into stone by pride and vanity.

"He thinks the enemy is afraid. He doesn't know that the Assyrian warriors are well trained: when they enter the army, they plant a tree, and every day they leap over the spot where the seed is buried. The seed becomes a shoot, and they leap over it. The shoot becomes a plant, and they go on jumping. They neither become annoyed nor find it a waste of time. Little by little, the tree grows, and the warriors leap higher. Patiently and with dedication, they're preparing to overcome obstacles.

"They're accustomed to recognizing a challenge when they see it. They've been observing us for months."

Elijah interrupted the governor.

"Then, in whose interest is war?"

"The high priest's. I saw that during the Assyrian prisoner's trial."

"For what reason?"

"I don't know. But he was shrewd enough to convince the commander and the people. Now the entire city is on his side, and I see only one way out of the difficult situation in which we find ourselves."

He paused for a long moment, then looked directly into the Israelite's eyes. "You."

The governor began pacing the chamber, his rapid speech betraying his nervousness.

"The merchants also desire peace, but they can do nothing. In any case, they are rich enough to install themselves in some other city or to wait until the conquerors begin buying their products. The rest of the populace have lost their senses and want us to attack an infinitely superior enemy. The only thing that can change their minds is a miracle."

Elijah became tense.

"A miracle?"

"You brought back a boy that death had already claimed. You've helped the people find their way, and though you are a foreigner you are loved by almost everyone."

"That was the situation until this morning," Elijah said. "But now it's changed; in the atmosphere you've just described, anyone who advocates peace will be considered a traitor."

"I don't want you to advocate anything. I want you to perform a miracle as great as the resurrection of that boy. Then you'll tell the people that peace is the only solution, and they'll listen to you. The high priest will lose completely whatever power he possesses."

There was a moment of silence. The governor continued.

"I am willing to make a pact: if you do what I'm asking, the religion of the One God will become obligatory in Akbar. You will please Him whom you serve, and I shall be able to negotiate terms of peace."

◆

ELIJAH CLIMBED THE STAIRS to his room in the upper story of the widow's house. At that moment he had in his hands an opportunity that no prophet had ever had before: to convert a Phoenician city. It would be the most painful way to show Jezebel that there was a price to pay for what she had done to his country.

He was excited by the governor's offer. He even thought of waking the woman who was sleeping downstairs but changed his mind; she must be dreaming about the beautiful afternoon they had spent together.

He called on his guardian angel. He appeared.

"You heard the governor's proposal," Elijah said. "This is a unique chance."

"Nothing is a unique chance," the angel replied. "The Lord giveth men many opportunities. And do not forget what was said: no further miracle will be permitted thee until thou returnest to the bosom of thy country."

Elijah lowered his head. At that moment the angel of the Lord appeared and hushed his guardian angel. And he said:

"Behold the next of thy miracles:

"Thou wilt gather the people together before the mountain. On one side, thou shalt order built an altar to Baal, and that a bullock be placed on it. On the other side, thou shalt raise an altar to the Lord thy God, and on it also place a bullock.

"And thou shalt say to the worshipers of Baal: invoke the name of your god, and I shall invoke the name of the Lord. Let them be first, and let them spend from morning until noon praying and calling on Baal to come forth and receive what is offered him.

"They will cry out aloud, and cut themselves with knives, asking that the bullock be received by their god, but nothing will happen.

"When they weary, thou shalt fill four barrels with water and pour it over thy bullock. Thou shalt do this a second time. And thou shalt do this still a third time. Then call upon the Lord of Abraham, Isaac, and Israel, asking Him to show His power to all.

"*At that moment, the Lord will send the fire from heaven and consume thy sacrifice.*"

Elijah knelt and gave thanks.

"However," continued the angel, "this miracle can be wrought but once in thy lifetime. Choose whether thou desirest to do it here, to avoid a battle, or in thy homeland, to free thy people from Jezebel."

And the angel of the Lord departed.

◆

THE WOMAN AWOKE EARLY and saw Elijah sitting in the doorway of the house. His eyes were deep in their sockets, like those of one who has not slept.

She would have liked to ask what had happened the night before, but she feared his response. It was possible that the sleepless night had been provoked by his talk with the governor and by the threat of war; but there might be another reason—the clay tablet she had given him. If so, and she raised the subject, she risked hearing that the love of a woman was not in accord with God's design.

She said only the words, "Come and eat something."

Her son awakened also. The three sat down at the table and ate.

"I should have liked to stay with you yesterday," Elijah said, "but the governor needed me."

"Do not concern yourself with him," she said, a calm feeling reentering her heart. "His family has ruled Akbar for generations, and he will know what to do in the face of the threat."

"I also spoke with an angel. And he demanded of me a very difficult decision."

"Nor should you be disturbed because of angels; perhaps it's better to believe that the gods change with the times. My ancestors worshiped the Egyptian gods, who had the forms of animals. Those gods went away, and until you arrived, I was brought up to make sacrifices to Asherat, El, Baal, and all the dwellers on the Fifth Mountain. Now I have known the Lord, but He too may leave us one day, and the next gods may be less demanding."

The boy asked for water. There was none.

"I'll go and fetch it," said Elijah.

"I want to go with you," the boy said.

They walked toward the well. On the way they passed the spot where the commander had since the early hours been training his soldiers.

"Let's watch for a while," said the boy. "I'll be a soldier when I grow up."

Elijah did as he asked.

"Which of us is best at using a sword?" asked one warrior.

"Go to the place where the spy was stoned yesterday," said the commander. "Pick up a stone and insult it."

"Why should I do that? The stone would not answer me back."

"Then attack it with your sword."

"My sword will break," said the soldier. "And that wasn't what I asked; I want to know who's the best at using a sword."

"The best is the one who's most like a rock," answered the commander. "Without drawing its blade, it proves that no one can defeat it."

"The governor is right: the commander is a wise man," thought Elijah. "But the greatest wisdom is blinded by the glare of vanity."

◆

THEY CONTINUED on their way. The boy asked why the soldiers were training so much.

"It's not just the soldiers, but your mother too, and I, and those who follow their heart. Everything in life demands training."

"Even being a prophet?"

"Even to understand angels. We so want to talk with them that we don't listen to what they're saying. It's not easy to listen: in our prayers we always try to say where we have erred, and what we should like to happen to us. But the Lord already knows all of this, and sometimes asks us only to hear what the Universe is telling us. And to be patient."

The boy looked at him in surprise. He probably understood nothing, but even so Elijah felt the need to continue the conversation. Perhaps when he came to manhood one of these words might assist him in a difficult situation.

"All life's battles teach us something, even those we lose. When you grow up, you'll discover that you have defended lies, deceived yourself, or suffered for foolishness. If you're a good warrior, you will not blame yourself for this, but neither will you allow your mistakes to repeat themselves."

He decided to speak no further; a boy of that age could not understand what he was saying. They walked slowly, and Elijah looked at the streets of the city that had sheltered him and was about to disappear. Everything depended on the decision he must make.

Akbar was more silent than usual. In the central square, people talked in hushed tones, as if fearful that the wind might carry their words to the Assyrian camp. The more elderly among them swore that nothing would happen, while the young were excited at the prospect of battle, and the merchants and artisans made plans to go to Sidon and Tyre until calm was restored.

"It is easy for them to leave," he thought. Merchants can transport their goods anywhere in the world. Artisans too can work, even in places where a strange language is spoken. "But I must have the Lord's permission."

◆

THEY CAME to the well, where they filled two vessels with water. Usually the place was crowded with people; women meeting to wash clothes, dye fabrics, and comment on everything that happened in the city. Nothing could be kept secret close to the well;

news about business, family betrayals, problems between neighbors, the intimate lives of the rulers—every matter, serious or superficial, was discussed, commented upon, criticized, or applauded there. Even during the months in which the enemy forces had grown unceasingly, Jezebel, the princess who had conquered the king of Israel, remained the favorite topic. People praised her boldness, her courage, and were certain that, should anything happen to the city, she would come back to her country to avenge it.

That morning, however, almost no one was there. The few women present said that it was necessary to go to the fields and harvest the largest possible amount of grain, for the Assyrians would soon close off the entrance and exit to the city. Two of them were making plans to go to the Fifth Mountain and offer sacrifices to the gods; they had no wish to see their sons die in combat.

"The high priest said that we can resist for many months," one woman commented to Elijah. "We need only to have the necessary courage to defend Akbar's honor and the gods will come to our aid."

The boy was frightened.

"Is the enemy going to attack?" he asked.

Elijah did not reply; it depended on the choice that the angel had offered him the night before.

"I'm afraid," the boy said insistently.

"That proves that you find joy in living. It's normal to feel fear at certain moments."

◆

ELIJAH AND THE BOY returned home before the morning was over. They found the woman ringed by small vessels with inks of various colors.

"I have to work," she said, looking at the unfinished letters and phrases. "Because of the drought, the city is full of dust. The brushes are always dirty, the ink mixes with dust, and everything becomes more difficult."

Elijah remained silent; he did not want to share his concerns with anyone. He sat in a corner of the downstairs room, absorbed in his thoughts. The boy went out to play with his friends.

"He needs silence," the woman said to herself and tried to concentrate on her work.

She took the rest of the morning to complete a few words that could have been written in half the time, and she felt guilt for not doing what was expected of her; after all, for the first time in her life she had the chance to support her family.

She returned to her work. She was using papyrus, a material that a trader on his way from Egypt had recently brought, asking her to write some commercial letters that he had to send to Damascus. The sheet was not of the best quality, and the ink blurred frequently. "Even with all these difficulties, it's better than drawing on clay."

Neighboring countries had the custom of sending their messages on clay tablets or on animal skins. Although their country was in decadence, with an obsolete script, the Egyptians had discovered a light, practical way of recording their commerce and their history; they cut into strips a plant that grew on the banks of the Nile and through a simple process glued the strips side by side, forming a yellowish sheet. Akbar had to import papyrus because it could not be grown in the valley. Though it was expensive, merchants preferred using it, for they could carry the written sheets in their pockets, which was impossible to do with clay tablets and animal skins.

"Everything is becoming simpler," she thought. A pity that the government's authorization was needed to use the Byblos alphabet on papyrus. Some outmoded law still obliged written texts to pass inspection by the Council of Akbar.

As soon as her work was done, she showed it to Elijah, who had been watching her the entire time without comment.

"Do you like the result?" she asked.

He seemed to come out of a trance.

"Yes, it's pretty," he replied, giving no mind to what he was saying.

He must be talking with the Lord. And she did not want to interrupt him. She left, to call the high priest.

When she returned with the high priest, Elijah was still in the same spot. The two men stared at each other. For a long time, neither spoke.

The high priest was the first to break the silence.

"You are a prophet, and speak with angels. I merely interpret the ancient laws, carry out rituals, and seek to defend my people from the errors they commit. Therefore I know this is not a struggle between men; it is a battle of gods—and I must not absent myself from it."

"I admire your faith, though you worship gods that do not exist," answered Elijah. "If the present situation is, as you say, worthy of a celestial battle, the Lord will use me as an instrument to defeat Baal and his companions on the Fifth Mountain. It would have been better for you to order my assassination."

"I thought of it. But it wasn't necessary; at the proper moment the gods acted in my favor."

Elijah did not reply. The high priest turned and picked up the papyrus on which the woman had just written her text.

"Well done," he commented. After reading it carefully, he took the ring from his finger, dipped it in one of the small vessels of ink, and applied his seal in the left corner. If anyone were found carrying a papyrus without the high priest's seal, he could be condemned to death.

"Why do you always have to do that?" she asked.

"Because these papyri transport ideas," he replied. "And ideas have power."

"They're just commercial transactions."

"But they could be battle plans. Or our secret prayers. Nowadays, with letters and papyrus, it has become a simple matter to steal the inspiration of a people. It is difficult to hide clay tablets, or animal skins, but the combination of papyrus and the alphabet of Byblos can bring an end to the civilization of any nation, and destroy the world."

A woman came running.

"Priest! Priest! Come see what's happening!"

Elijah and the widow followed him. People were coming from every corner, heading for the same place; the air was close to unbreathable from the dust they raised. Children ran ahead, laughing and shouting. The adults walked slowly, in silence.

When they arrived at the southern gate to the city, a small multitude was already gathered there. The high priest pushed his way through the crowd and came upon the reason for the confusion.

A sentinel of Akbar was kneeling, his arms spread, his hands tied to a large piece of wood on his shoulders. His clothes were in tatters, and his left eye had been gouged out by a small tree branch.

On his chest, written with slashes of a knife, were some Assyrian characters. The high priest understood Egyptian, but the Assyrian language was not important enough to be learned and memorized; it was necessary to ask the help of a trader who was at the scene.

"'*We declare war*,'" the man translated.

The onlookers spoke not a word. Elijah could see panic written on their faces.

"Give me your sword," the high priest said to one of the soldiers.

The soldier obeyed. The high priest asked that the governor and the commander be notified of what had happened. Then, with a swift blow, he plunged the blade into the kneeling sentinel's heart.

The man moaned and fell to the ground. He was dead, free of the pain and shame of having allowed himself to be captured.

"Tomorrow I shall go to the Fifth Mountain to offer sacrifices," he told the frightened people. "And the gods will once again remember us."

Before leaving, he turned to Elijah.

"You see it with your own eyes. The heavens are still helping."

"One question, nothing more," said Elijah. "Why do you wish to see your people sacrificed?"

"Because it is what must be done to kill an idea."

After seeing him talk with the woman that morning, Elijah had understood what that idea was: the alphabet.

"It is too late. Already it spreads throughout the world, and the Assyrians cannot conquer the whole of the earth."

"And who says they cannot? After all, the gods of the Fifth Mountain are on the side of their armies."

◆

FOR HOURS HE WALKED the valley, as he had done the afternoon before. He knew there would be at least one more afternoon and night of peace: no war was fought in darkness, because the soldiers could not distinguish the enemy. That night, he knew, the Lord was giving him the chance to change the destiny of the city that had taken him into its bosom.

"Solomon would know what to do," he told his angel. "And David, and Moses, and Isaac. They were men the Lord trusted, but I am merely an indecisive servant. The Lord has given me a choice that should be His."

"The history of our ancestors seemeth to be full of the right men in the right places," answered the angel. "Do not believe it: the Lord demandeth of people only that which is within the possibilities of each of them."

"Then He has made a mistake with me."

"Whatever affliction that cometh, finally goeth away. Such are the glories and tragedies of the world."

"I shall not forget that," Elijah said. "But when they go away, the tragedies leave behind eternal marks, while the glories leave useless memories."

The angel made no reply.

"Why, during all this time I have been in Akbar, could I not find allies to work toward peace? What importance has a solitary prophet?"

"What importance hath the sun, in its solitary travel through the heavens? What importance hath a mountain rising in the middle of a valley? What importance hath an isolated well? Yet it is they that indicate the road the caravan is to follow."

"My heart drowns in sorrow," said Elijah, kneeling and extending his arms to heaven. "Would that I could die here and now, and never have my hands stained with the blood of my people, or a foreign people. Look behind you. What do you see?"

"Thou knowest that I am blind," said the angel. "Because mine eyes still retain the light of the Lord's glory, I can perceive nothing else. I can see only what thy heart telleth me. I can see only the vibrations of the dangers that threaten thee. I cannot know what lieth behind thee . . . "

"Then I'll tell you: there lies Akbar. Seen at this time of day, with the afternoon sun lighting its profile, it's lovely. I have grown accustomed to its streets and walls, to its generous and hospitable folk. Though the city's inhabitants are still prisoners of commerce and superstition, their hearts are as pure as any nation on earth. With them I have learned much that I did not know; in return, I have listened to their laments and—inspired by God—have been able to resolve their internal conflicts. Many times have I been at risk, and someone has always come to my aid. Why must I choose between saving this city and redeeming my people?"

"Because a man must choose," answered the angel. "Therein lieth his strength: the power of his decisions."

"It is a difficult choice; it demands that I accept the death of one people to save another."

"Even more difficult is defining a path for oneself. He who maketh no choice is dead in the eyes of the Lord, though he go on breathing and walking in the streets.

"Moreover," the angel continued, "no one dieth. The arms

The Fifth Mountain

of eternity open for every soul, and each one will carry on his task. There is a reason for everything under the sun."

Elijah again raised his arms to the heavens.

"My people fell away from the Lord because of a woman's beauty. Phoenicia may be destroyed because a priest thinks that writing is a threat to the gods. Why does He who made the world prefer to use tragedy to write the book of fate?"

Elijah's cries echoed through the valley to return to his ears.

"Thou knowest not whereof thou speakest," the angel replied. "There is no tragedy, only the unavoidable. Everything hath its reason for being: thou needest only distinguish what is temporary from what is lasting."

"What is temporary?" asked Elijah.

"The unavoidable."

"And what is lasting?"

"The lessons of the unavoidable."

Saying this, the angel disappeared.

That night, at the evening meal, Elijah told the woman and the boy, "Prepare your things. We may depart at any moment."

"You haven't slept for two days," said the woman. "An emissary from the governor was here this afternoon, asking for you to go to the palace. I said you were in the valley and would spend the night there."

"You did well," he replied, going straightway to his room and falling into a deep sleep.

HE WAS AWAKENED THE NEXT MORNING BY THE SOUND of musical instruments. When he went downstairs to see what was happening, the boy was already at the door.

"Look!" he said, his eyes gleaming with excitement. "It's war!"

A battalion of soldiers, imposing in their battle gear and armaments, was marching toward the southern gate of Akbar. A group of musicians followed them, marking the battalion's pace to the beat of drums.

"Yesterday you were afraid," Elijah told the boy.

"I didn't know we had so many soldiers. Our warriors are the best!"

He left the boy and went into the street; he must find the governor at any cost. The other inhabitants of the city had been awakened by the sound of the war anthems and were enthralled;

for the first time in their lives they were seeing the march of an organized battalion in its military uniforms, its lances and shields reflecting the first rays of dawn. The commander had achieved an enviable feat; he had prepared his army without anyone becoming aware of it, and now—or so Elijah feared—he could make everyone believe that victory over the Assyrians was possible.

He pushed his way through the soldiers and came to the front of the column. There, mounted on horses, the commander and the governor were leading the march.

"We have an agreement!" said Elijah, running to the governor's side. "I can perform a miracle!"

The governor made no reply. The garrison marched past the city wall and into the valley.

"You know this army is an illusion!" Elijah insisted. "The Assyrians have a five-to-one advantage, and they are experienced warriors! Don't allow Akbar to be destroyed!"

"What do you desire of me?" the governor asked, without halting his steed. "Last night I sent an emissary so we could talk, and they said you were out of the city. What else could I do?"

"Facing the Assyrians in the open field is suicide! You know that!"

The commander was listening to the conversation, making no comment. He had already discussed his strategy with the governor; the Israelite prophet would have a surprise.

Elijah ran alongside the horses, not knowing exactly what he should do. The column of soldiers left the city, heading toward the middle of the valley.

"Help me, Lord," he thought. "Just as Thou stopped the sun to help Joshua in combat, stop time and let me convince the governor of his error."

As soon as he thought this, the commander shouted, "Halt!"

"Perhaps it's a sign," Elijah told himself. "I must take advantage of it."

The soldiers formed two lines of engagement, like human walls. Their shields were firmly anchored in the earth, their swords pointing outward.

"You believe you are looking at Akbar's warriors," the governor said to Elijah.

"I'm looking at young men who laugh in the face of death," was the reply.

"Know then that what we have here is only a battalion. The greater part of our men are in the city, on top of the walls. We have placed there caldrons of boiling oil ready to be poured on the heads of anyone trying to scale them.

"We have stores divided among several locations, so that flaming arrows cannot do away with our food supply. According to the commander's calculations, we can hold out for almost two months against a siege. While the Assyrians were making ready, so too were we."

"I was never told this," Elijah said.

"Remember this: even having helped the people of Akbar, you are still a foreigner, and some in the military could mistake you for a spy."

"But you wished for peace!"

"Peace is still possible, even after combat begins. But now we shall negotiate under conditions of equality."

The governor related that messengers had been dispatched to Sidon and Tyre advising of the gravity of their position. It had been difficult for him to ask for help; others might think him incapable of controlling the situation. But he had concluded that this was the only solution.

The commander had developed an ingenious plan; as soon as combat began, he would return to the city to organize the resistance. The troops in the field were to kill as many of the enemy as possible, then withdraw to the mountains. They knew the valley better than anyone and could attack the Assyrians in small skirmishes, thus reducing the pressure of the siege.

Relief would come soon, and the Assyrian army would be decimated. "We can resist for sixty days, but that will not be necessary," the governor told Elijah.

"But many will die."

"We are all in the presence of death. And no one is afraid, not even I."

The governor was surprised at his own courage. He had never before been in a battle, and as the moment of combat drew nearer, he had made plans to flee the city. That morning he had agreed with some of his most faithful friends on the best means of retreat. He could not go to Sidon or Tyre, where he would be considered a traitor, but Jezebel would receive him because she needed men she could trust.

But when he stepped onto the field of battle, he had seen in the soldiers' eyes an immense joy, as if they had trained their entire lives for an objective and the great moment had finally come.

"Fear exists until the moment when the unavoidable happens," he told Elijah. "After that, we must waste none of our energy on it."

Elijah was confused. He felt the same way, though he was ashamed to recognize it; he recalled the boy's excitement when the troops had marched past.

"Away with you," the governor said. "You're a foreigner, unarmed, and have no need to fight for something you do not believe in."

Elijah did not move.

"They will come," said the commander. "You were caught by surprise, but we are prepared."

Even so, Elijah remained where he stood.

They scanned the horizon: no dust. The Assyrian army was not on the move.

The soldiers in the first rank held their spears firmly, pointed forward; the bowmen had their strings half-drawn, ready to loose their arrows at the commander's order. A few men slashed at the air with their swords to keep their muscles warm.

"Everything is ready," the commander repeated. "They are going to attack."

Elijah noticed the euphoria in his voice. He must be eager for the battle to begin, eager to demonstrate his bravery. Beyond a doubt he was imagining the Assyrian warriors, the sword blows, the shouting and confusion, and picturing himself being remembered by the Phoenician priests as an example of efficiency and courage.

The governor interrupted his thoughts.

"They're not moving."

Elijah remembered what he had asked of the Lord, for the sun to stand still in the heavens as He had done for Joshua. He tried to talk with his angel but did not hear his voice.

Little by little the spearmen lowered their weapons, the archers relaxed the tension on their bowstrings, the swordsmen replaced their weapons in their scabbards. The burning sun of midday arrived; several warriors fainted from the heat. Even so, for the rest of the day the detachment remained at readiness.

When the sun set, the warriors returned to Akbar; they appeared disappointed at having survived another day.

Elijah alone stayed behind in the valley. He had been wandering about for some time when the light appeared. The angel of the Lord was before him.

"God hath heard thy prayers," the angel said. "And hath seen the torment in thy soul."

Elijah turned to the heavens and gave thanks for the blessing.

"The Lord is the source of all glory and all power. He stopped the Assyrian army."

"No," the angel replied. "Thou hast said that the choice must be His. And He hath made the choice for thee."

"Let's go," the woman told her son.

"I don't want to go," the boy replied. "I'm proud of Akbar's soldiers."

His mother bade him gather his belongings. "Take only what you can carry," she said.

"You forget we're poor, and I don't have much."

Elijah went up to his room. He looked about him, as if for the first and last time; he quickly descended and stood watching the widow store her inks.

"Thank you for taking me with you," she said. "I was only fifteen when I married, and I had no idea what life was. Our families had arranged everything; I had been raised since childhood for that moment and carefully prepared to help my husband in all circumstances."

"Did you love him?"

"I taught my heart to do so. Because there was no choice, I convinced myself that it was the best way. When I lost my husband, I resigned myself to the sameness of day and night; I asked the gods of the Fifth Mountain—in those times I still believed in them—to take me as soon as my son could live on his own.

"That was when you appeared. I've told you this once before, and I want to repeat it now: from that day on, I began to notice the beauty of the valley, the dark outline of the mountains projected against the sky, the moon ever-changing shape so the wheat could grow. Many nights while you slept I walked about Akbar, listening to the cries of newborn infants, the songs of men who had been drinking after work, the firm steps of the sentinels on the city walls. How many times had I seen that landscape without noticing how beautiful it was? How many times had I looked at the sky without seeing how deep it is? How many times had I heard the sounds of Akbar around me without understanding that they were part of my life?

"I once again felt an immense will to live. You told me to study the characters of Byblos, and I did. I thought only of pleasing you, but I came to care deeply about what I was doing, and I discovered something: *the meaning of my life was whatever I wanted it to be.*"

Elijah stroked her hair. It was the first time he had done so.

"Why haven't you always been like this?" she asked.

"Because I was afraid. But today, waiting for the battle to start, I heard the governor's words, and I thought of you. Fear reaches only to the point where the unavoidable begins; from there on, it loses its meaning. And all we have left is the hope that we are making the right decision."

"I'm ready," she said.

"We shall return to Israel. The Lord has told me what I must do, and so I shall. Jezebel will be removed from power."

She said nothing. Like all Phoenician women, she was proud of her princess. When they arrived there, she would try to convince the man at her side to change his mind.

"It will be a long journey, and we shall find no rest until I have done what He has asked of me," said Elijah, as if guessing her thoughts. "Still, your love will be my mainstay, and in the moments I grow weary in the battles in His name, I can find repose in your arms."

The boy appeared, carrying a small bag on his shoulder. Elijah took it and told the woman, "The hour has come. As you traverse the streets of Akbar, remember each house, each sound. For you will never again see them."

"I was born in Akbar," she said. "The city will forever remain in my heart."

Hearing this, the boy vowed to himself never to forget his mother's words. If someday he could return, he would look upon the city as if seeing her face.

◆

IT WAS ALREADY DARK when the high priest arrived at the foot of the Fifth Mountain. In his right hand he held a staff; in his left he carried a large sack.

From the sack he took the sacred oil and anointed his forehead and wrists. Then, using the staff, he drew in the sand a bull and a panther, the symbols of the God of the Storm and of the Great Goddess. He said the ritual prayers; finally he opened his arms to heaven to receive the divine revelation.

The gods spoke no more. They had said all they wished to say and now demanded only the carrying out of the rites. The prophets had disappeared everywhere in the world, save in Israel, a backward, superstitious country that still believed men could communicate with the creators of the Universe.

He recalled that generations before, Sidon and Tyre had traded with a king of Jerusalem called Solomon. He was building a great temple and desired to adorn it with the best the world offered; he had commanded that cedars be bought from Phoenicia, which they called Lebanon. The king of Tyre had provided the necessary materials and had received in exchange twenty cities in Galilee, but was not pleased with them. Solomon had then helped him to construct his first ships, and now Phoenicia had the largest merchant fleet in the world.

At that time, Israel was still a great nation, despite worshiping a single god whose name was not even known and who was usually called just "the Lord." A princess of Sidon had succeeded in returning Solomon to the true faith, and he had erected an altar to the gods of the Fifth Mountain. The Israelites insisted that "the Lord" had punished the wisest of their kings, bringing about the wars that had threatened his reign.

His son Rehoboam, however, carried on the worship that his father had initiated. He ordered two golden calves to be made, and the people of Israel worshiped them. It was then that the prophets appeared and began a ceaseless struggle against the rulers.

Jezebel was right: the only way to keep the true faith alive was by doing away with the prophets. Although she was a gentle woman, brought up in the way of tolerance and of horror at the thought of war, she knew that there comes a moment when violence is the only answer. The blood that now stained her hands would be forgiven by the gods she served.

"Soon, my hands too will be stained with blood," the high priest told the silent mountain before him. "Just as the prophets are the curse of Israel, writing is the curse of Phoenicia. Both bring about an evil beyond redress, and both must be stopped while it is still possible. The god of weather must not desert us now."

He was concerned about what had happened that morning; the enemy army had not attacked. The god of weather had abandoned Phoenicia in the past because he had become irritated at its inhabitants. As a consequence, the light of the lamps had stilled, the lambs and cows had abandoned their young, the wheat and barley had failed to ripen. The Sun god commanded that important beings be sent to search for him—the eagle and the God of the Storm—but no one succeeded in finding him. Finally, the Great Goddess sent a bee, which found him asleep in a forest and stung him. He awoke furious and began to destroy everything around him. It was necessary to bind him and remove the wrath from his soul, but from that time onward, all returned to normal.

If he decided to leave again, the battle would not take place. The Assyrians would remain permanently in the entrance to the valley, and Akbar would continue to exist.

"Courage is fear that prays," he said. "That is why I am here, because I cannot vacillate at the moment of combat. I must show the warriors of Akbar that there is a reason to defend the city. It is neither the well, nor the marketplace, nor the governor's palace. We shall confront the Assyrian army because we must set the example."

The Assyrian triumph would end the threat of the alphabet for all time to come. The conquerors would impose their language and their customs, but they would go on worshiping the same gods on the Fifth Mountain; that was what truly mattered.

"In the future, our navigators will take to other lands the feats of our warriors. The priests will recall the names and the date when Akbar attempted to resist the Assyrian invasion. Painters will draw Egyptian characters on papyrus; the scribes of Byblos will be dead. The sacred texts will continue only in the hands of those born to study them. Then the later generations will try to imitate what we have done, and we shall build a better world.

"But now," he continued, "we must first lose this battle. We shall fight bravely, but our situation is inferior, and we shall die with glory."

At that moment the high priest listened to the night and saw that he was right. The silence anticipated the moment of an important battle, but the inhabitants of Akbar were misinterpreting it; they had laid down their weapons and were amusing themselves at precisely the moment when they had need of vigilance. They paid no heed to nature's example: the animals fell silent when danger was at hand.

"Let the gods' designs be fulfilled. May the heavens not fall upon the earth, for we have acted rightly; we have obeyed tradition," he concluded.

ELIJAH, THE WOMAN, AND THE BOY WENT IN A WESTERLY direction, toward Israel; they did not need to pass near the Assyrian encampment because it was located to the south. The full moon made the walk easier but also cast strange shadows and sinister forms on the rocks and stones of the valley.

In the midst of the darkness, the angel of the Lord appeared. He bore a sword of fire in his right hand.

"Whither goest thou?" he asked.

"To Israel," Elijah answered.

"Hath the Lord summoned thee?"

"I know the miracle that God expects me to perform. And now I know where I am to execute it."

"Hath the Lord summoned thee?" repeated the angel.

Elijah remained silent.

"Hath the Lord summoned thee?" asked the angel for the third time.

"No."

"Then return to the place whence thou comest, for thou hast yet to fulfill thy destiny. The Lord hath still to summon thee."

"If nothing else, permit them to leave, for they have no reason to remain," implored Elijah.

But the angel was no longer there. Elijah dropped the bag he was carrying, sat in the middle of the road, and wept bitterly.

"What happened?" asked the woman and the boy, who had seen nothing.

"We're going back," he said. "Such is the Lord's desire."

◆

HE WAS NOT ABLE to sleep well. He awoke in the night and sensed the tension in the air around him; an evil wind blew through the streets, sowing fear and distrust.

"In the love of a woman, I have discovered the love for all creatures," he prayed silently. "I need her. I know that the Lord will not forget that I am one of His instruments, perhaps the weakest of those He has chosen. Help me, O Lord, because I must repose calmly amidst the battles."

He recalled the governor's comment about the uselessness of fear. Despite that, sleep eluded him. "I need energy and tranquillity; give me rest while it is still possible."

He thought of summoning his angel and talking with him for

a while, but knowing he might be told things he had no wish to hear, he changed his mind. To relax, he went downstairs; the bags that the woman had prepared for their flight had not been undone.

He considered returning to his room. He remembered what the Lord had told Moses: *"And what man is there that hath betrothed a wife, and hath not taken her? Let him go and return unto his house, lest he die in the battle, and another man take her."*

They had not yet known each other. But it had been a wearying night, and this was not the moment to do so.

He decided to unpack the bags and return everything to its place. He discovered that, besides the few clothes she possessed, she was carrying the instruments for drawing the characters of Byblos.

He picked up a stylus, moistened a small clay tablet, and began to sketch a few letters; he had learned to write by watching the woman as she worked.

"What a simple and ingenious thing," he thought, in an effort to turn his mind to other concerns. Often, on his way to the well for water, he had heard the women commenting, "The Greeks stole our most important invention," but Elijah knew it was not that way: the adaptation they had made by including vowels had transformed the alphabet into something that the peoples of all nations could use. Furthermore, they called their collections of parchments *biblia*, in honor of the city where the invention had occurred.

The Greek *biblia* were written on animal hides. Elijah felt this was a very fragile way of storing words; hides were less resistant than clay tablets and could be easily stolen. Papyrus came apart after some handling and was destroyed by water. "*Biblia* and papyrus will not last; only clay tablets are destined to remain forever," he reflected.

If Akbar survived for a time longer, he would recommend that the governor order his country's entire history written on clay tablets and stored in a special room, so that generations yet to come might consult them. In this way, if one day the priests of Phoenicia, who kept in their memory the history of their people, were decimated, the feats of warriors and poets would not be forgotten.

He amused himself for some time by writing the same letters but by ordering them differently, forming several words. He was enchanted with the result. The task relaxed him, and he returned to his bed.

◆

HE AWOKE some time later at the sound of the door to his room crashing to the floor.

"It's not a dream. It's not the armies of the Lord in combat."

Shadows came from all sides, screaming like madmen in a language he did not understand.

"The Assyrians."

Other doors fell, walls were leveled by powerful hammer blows, the shouts of the invaders mixed with cries for help rising from the square. He attempted to stand, but one of the shadows knocked him to the ground. A muffled sound shook the floor below.

"Fire," Elijah thought. "They've set the house on fire."

"It's you," he heard someone saying in Phoenician. "You're the leader. Hiding like a coward in a woman's house."

He looked at the face of the person who had just spoken; flames lit the room, and he could see a man with a long beard, in a military uniform. Yes, the Assyrians had come.

"You invaded at night?" he asked, disoriented.

The man did not respond. Elijah saw the flash of swords drawn from their scabbards, and one of the warriors slashed his right arm.

Elijah closed his eyes; the scenes of an entire lifetime passed before him in a fraction of a second. He was once again playing in the street of the city of his birth, traveling to Jerusalem for the first time, smelling the odor of cut wood in the carpenter's shop, marveling at the vastness of the sea and at the garments people wore in the great cities of the coast. He saw himself walking the valleys and mountains of the Promised Land, remembered when he first saw Jezebel, who seemed like a young girl and charmed all who came near. He witnessed a second time the massacre of the prophets, heard anew the voice of the Lord ordering him into the desert. He saw again the eyes of the woman who awaited him at the gates of Zarephath, which its inhabitants called Akbar, and understood that he had loved her from the first moment. Once more he climbed the Fifth Mountain, brought a child back to life, and was welcomed by the people as a sage and a judge. He looked at the heavens, where the constellations were rapidly changing position, was dazzled by the moon that displayed its four phases in a single instant, felt heat, cold, fall and spring, experienced the rain and the lightning's flash.

Clouds swept past in millions of different shapes, and the water of rivers again ran in their beds. He relived the day that he had seen the first Assyrian tent being erected, then the second, then several, many, the angels that came and went, the fiery sword on the road to Israel, sleepless nights, drawings on clay tablets, and—

He was back in the present. He thought about what was happening on the floor below; he had to save the widow and her son at any cost.

"Fire!" he told one of the enemy soldiers. "The house is on fire!"

He was not afraid; his only concern was for the widow and her child. Someone pushed his head against the floor, and he felt the taste of earth in his mouth. He kissed it, told it how much he loved it, and explained that he had done everything possible to avoid what was happening. He tried to wrest free of his captors, but someone had his foot on his chest.

"She must have fled," he thought. "They wouldn't harm a defenseless woman."

A deep calm took hold of his heart. Perhaps the Lord had come to realize that he was the wrong man and had found another prophet to rescue Israel from sin. Death had finally come, in the way he had hoped, through martyrdom. He accepted his fate and waited for the fatal blow.

Seconds went by; the voices were still shouting, blood still ran from his wound, but the fatal blow had not come.

"Ask them to kill me at once!" he shouted, knowing that at least one of them spoke his language.

No one heeded his words. They were arguing heatedly, as if something had gone wrong. Some of the soldiers began kicking him, and for the first time Elijah noticed the instinct for survival reasserting itself. This created in him a sensation of panic.

"I can't wish for life any longer," he thought desperately. "Because I'm not leaving this room alive."

But nothing happened. The world seemed to be suspended endlessly in that confusion of shouts, noises, and dust. Perhaps the Lord had done as He had with Joshua and time had stood still amid the combat.

That was when he heard the woman's screams from below. With an effort surpassing human strength, Elijah pushed aside two of the guards and struggled to his feet, but he was quickly struck down; a soldier kicked him in the head, and he fainted.

◆

A FEW MINUTES LATER he recovered consciousness. The Assyrians had dragged him into the street.

Still dizzy, he raised his head; every house in the neighborhood was in flames.

"An innocent, helpless woman is caught in there! Save her!"

Cries, people running in every direction, confusion everywhere. He tried to rise but was struck down again.

"Lord, Thou canst do with me as Thou wilt, for I have dedicated my life and my death to Thy cause," Elijah prayed. "But save the woman who took me in!"

Someone raised him by his arms.

"Come and see," said the Assyrian officer who knew his language. "You deserve it."

Two guards seized him and pushed him toward the door. The house was rapidly being devoured by flames, and the light from the fire illuminated everything around it. He heard cries coming from all sides: children sobbing, old men begging for forgiveness, desperate women searching for their children. But he had ears only for the pleas for help of the woman who had afforded him shelter.

"What is happening? A woman and child are inside! Why have you done this to them?"

"Because she tried to hide the governor of Akbar."

"I'm not the governor! You're making a terrible mistake!"

The Assyrian officer pushed him toward the door. The ceiling had collapsed in the fire, and the woman was half-buried in the debris. Elijah could see only her arm, moving desperately from side to side. She was asking for help, begging them not to let her be burned alive.

"Why spare me," he implored, "and do this to her?"

"We're not going to spare you, but we want you to suffer as much as possible. Our general died without honor, stoned to death, in front of the city walls. He came in search of life and was condemned to death. Now you will have the same fate."

Elijah struggled desperately to free himself, but the guards carried him away. They passed through the streets of Akbar, in infernal heat; the soldiers were sweating heavily, and some of them appeared shocked at the scene they had just witnessed. Elijah thrashed about, clamoring against the heavens, but the Assyrians were as silent as the Lord Himself.

They arrived at the square. Most of the buildings in the city were ablaze, and the sound of flames mingled with the cries of Akbar's inhabitants.

"How good that death still exists."

Since that day in the stable, how often Elijah had thought this!

The corpses of Akbar's warriors, most of them without uniforms, were spread out on the ground. He saw people running in every direction, not knowing where they were going, not knowing what they sought, guided by nothing more than the necessity of pretending they were doing something, fighting against death and destruction.

"Why do they do that?" he thought. "Don't they see the city is in the hands of the enemy and there is nowhere to flee?" Everything had happened very quickly. The Assyrians had taken advantage of their large superiority in numbers and had been able to spare their warriors from combat. Akbar's soldiers had been exterminated almost without a struggle.

They stopped in the middle of the square. Elijah was made to kneel on the ground and his hands were tied. He no longer heard the woman's screams; perhaps she had died quickly, without going through the slow torture of being burned alive. The Lord had her in His hands. And she was carrying her son at her bosom.

Another group of Assyrian soldiers brought a prisoner whose face was disfigured by numerous blows. Even so, Elijah recognized the commander.

"Long live Akbar!" he shouted. "Long life to Phoenicia and its warriors, who engage the enemy by day! Death to the cowards who attack in darkness!"

He barely had time to finish the phrase. An Assyrian general's sword descended, and the commander's head rolled along the ground.

"Now it is my turn," Elijah told himself. "I'll meet her again in paradise, where we shall stroll hand in hand."

At that moment, a man approached and began to argue with the officers. He was an inhabitant of Akbar who was wont to attend the meetings in the square. Elijah recalled having helped him resolve a serious dispute with a neighbor.

The Assyrians were arguing among themselves, their words growing louder and louder, and pointing at him. The man kneeled, kissed the feet of one of them, extended his hand toward the Fifth Mountain, and wept like a child. The invaders' fury appeared to subside.

The discussion seemed to go on endlessly. The man implored and wept the entire time, pointing to Elijah and to the house where the governor lived. The soldiers appeared dissatisfied with the conversation.

Finally, the officer who spoke his language approached.

"Our spy," he said, indicating the man, "says that we are mistaken. It was he who gave us the plans to the city, and we have confidence in what he says. It's not you we wish to kill."

He pushed him with his foot. Elijah fell to the ground.

"He says you would go to Israel and remove the princess who usurped the throne. Is that true?"

Elijah did not answer.

"Tell me if it's true," the officer insisted. "And you can leave here and return to your dwelling in time to save that woman and her son."

"Yes, it's true," he said. Perhaps the Lord had listened to him and would help him to save them.

"We could take you captive to Sidon and Tyre," the officer continued. "But we still have many battles before us, and you'd be a weight on our backs. We could demand a ransom for you, but from whom? You're a foreigner even in your own country."

The officer put his foot on Elijah's face.

"You're useless. You're no good to the enemy and no good to friends. Just like your city; it's not worth leaving part of our army here, to keep it under our rule. After we conquer the coastal cities Akbar will be ours in any case."

"I have one question," Elijah said. "Just one question."

The officer looked at him warily.

"Why did you attack at night? Don't you know that wars are fought by day?"

"We did not break the law; there is no custom that forbids it," answered the officer. "And we had a long time to become familiar with the terrain. All of you were so preoccupied with custom that you forgot that times change."

Without a further word, the group left him. The spy approached and untied his hands.

"I promised myself that I would one day repay your generosity; I have kept my word. When the Assyrians entered the palace, one of the servants told them that the man they were looking for had taken refuge in the widow's house. While they went there, the real governor was able to flee."

Elijah was not listening. Fire crackled everywhere, and the screams continued.

In the midst of the confusion, it was evident that one group still maintained discipline; obeying an invisible order, the Assyrians were silently withdrawing.

The battle of Akbar was over.

◆

"SHE'S DEAD," he told himself. "I don't want to go there, for she is dead. Or she was saved by a miracle and will come looking for me."

His heart nevertheless bade him rise to his feet and go to the house where they lived. Elijah struggled with himself; at that moment, more than a woman's love was at stake—his entire life, his faith in the Lord's designs, the departure from the city of his birth, the idea that he had a mission and was capable of completing it.

He looked about him, searching for a sword with which to take his own life, but with the Assyrians had gone every weapon in Akbar. He thought of throwing himself onto the flames of the burning houses, but he feared the pain.

For some moments he stood paralyzed. Little by little, he began recovering his awareness of the situation in which he found himself. The woman and her child must have already left this world, but he must bury them in accord with custom. At that moment the Lord's work—whether or not He existed—was his only succor. After finishing his religious duty, he would yield to pain and doubt.

Moreover, there was a possibility that they still lived. He could not remain there, doing nothing.

"I don't want to see their burned faces, the skin falling from their flesh. Their souls are already running free in heaven."

◆

NEVERTHELESS, HE BEGAN walking toward the house, choking and blinded by the smoke that prevented his finding his way. He gradually began to comprehend the situation in the city. Although the enemy had withdrawn, panic was mounting in an alarming manner. People continued to wander aimlessly, weeping, petitioning the gods on behalf of their dead.

He looked for someone to help him. A lone man was in sight, in a total state of shock; his mind seemed distant.

"It's best to go straightway and not ask for help." He knew Akbar as if it were his native city and was able to orient himself, even without recognizing many of the places that he was accustomed to passing. In the street the cries he heard were now more coherent. The people were beginning to understand that a tragedy had taken place and that it was necessary to react.

"There's a wounded man here!" said one.

"We need more water! We're not going to be able to control the fire!" said another.

"Help me! My husband is trapped!"

He came to the place where, many months before, he had been received and given lodging as a friend. An old woman was sitting in the middle of the street, almost in front of the house, completely naked. Elijah tried to help her but was pushed away.

"She's dying!" the old woman cried. "Do something! Take that wall off her!"

And she began screaming hysterically. Elijah took her by the arms and shoved her aside, for the noise she was making prevented his hearing the widow's moans. Everything around him was total destruction—the roof and walls had collapsed, and it was difficult to recognize where he had last seen her. The flames had died down but the heat was still unbearable; he stepped over the rubble covering the floor and went toward the place where the woman's bedroom had been.

Despite the confusion outside, he was able to make out a moan. It was her voice.

He instinctively shook the dust from his garments, as if trying to improve his appearance. He remained silent, trying to concentrate. He heard the crackling of the fire, the cries for help from people buried in the neighboring houses, and felt the urge to tell them to be silent because he must discover where the woman and her son were. After a long time, he heard the sound again; someone was scratching on the wood beneath his feet.

He fell to his knees and began digging like one possessed. He removed the dirt, stones, and wood. Finally, his hand touched something warm: it was blood.

"Please, don't die," he said.

"Leave the rubble over me," he heard her voice say. "I don't want you to see my face. Go and help my son."

He continued to dig, and she repeated, "Go and find the body of my son. Please, do as I ask."

Elijah's head fell against his chest, and he began weeping softly.

"I don't know where he's buried," he said. "Please, don't go; how I long to have you remain with me. I need you to teach me how to love; my heart is ready now."

"Before you arrived, for so many years I called out to death. It must have heard and come looking for me."

She moaned. Elijah bit his lips but said nothing. Someone touched his shoulder.

Startled, he turned and saw the boy. He was covered with dust and soot but appeared unhurt.

"Where is my mother?" he asked.

"I'm here, my son," answered the voice from beneath the ruins. "Are you injured?"

The boy began to cry. Elijah took him in his arms.

"You're crying, my son," said the voice, ever weaker. "Don't do that. Your mother took a long time to learn that life has meaning; I hope I have been able to teach it to you. In what condition is the city where you were born?"

Elijah and the boy remained silent, each clinging to the other.

"It's fine," Elijah lied. "A few warriors died, but the Assyrians have withdrawn. They were after the governor, to avenge the death of one of their generals."

Again, silence. And again her voice, still weaker than before.

"Tell me that my city is safe."

He knew that she would be gone at any moment.

"The city is whole. And your son is well."

"What about you?"

"I have survived."

He knew that with these words he was liberating her soul and allowing her to die in peace.

"Ask my son to kneel," the woman said after a time. "And I want you to swear to me, in the name of the Lord thy God."

"Whatever you want. Anything that you want."

"You once told me that the Lord is everywhere, and I believed you. You said that souls don't go to the top of the Fifth Mountain, and I also believed what you said. But you didn't explain where they go.

"This is the oath: you two will not weep for me, and each

will take care of the other until the Lord allows each of you to follow his path. From this moment on, my soul will become one with all I have known on this earth: I am the valley, the mountains that surround it, the city, the people walking in its streets. I am its wounded and its beggars, its soldiers, its priests, its merchants, its nobles. I am the ground that they tread, and the well that slakes each one's thirst.

"Don't weep for me, for there is no reason to be sad. From this moment on, I am Akbar, and the city is beautiful."

The silence of death descended, and the wind ceased to blow. Elijah no longer heard the cries outside or the flames crackling in neighboring houses; he heard only the silence and could almost touch it in its intensity.

Then Elijah led the boy away, rent his own garments, turned to the heavens, and bellowed with all the strength of his lungs, "O Lord my God! For Thy cause have I left Israel and cannot offer Thee my blood as did the prophets who remained there. I have been called a coward by my friends and a traitor by my enemies.

"For Thy cause have I eaten only what crows brought me and have crossed the desert to Zarephath, which its inhabitants call Akbar. Guided by Thy hand, I met a woman; guided by Thee, my heart learned to love her. But at no time did I forget my true mission; during all the days I spent here I was always ready to depart.

"Beautiful Akbar is in ruins, and the woman who trusted me lies beneath them. Where have I sinned, O Lord? At what moment have I strayed from what Thou desirest of me? If Thou art discontent with me, why hast Thou not taken me from this world? Instead, Thou hast afflicted yet again those who succored me and loved me.

"I do not understand Thy designs. I see no justice in Thy acts. In bearing the suffering Thou hast imposed on me, I am sorely wanting. Remove Thyself from my life, for I too am reduced to ruins, fire, and dust."

Amidst the fire and desolation, the light appeared to Elijah. And the angel of the Lord was before him.

"Why are you here?" asked Elijah. "Don't you see that it is too late?"

"I have come to say that once again the Lord hath heard thy prayer and thy petition will be granted thee. No more shalt thou hear thy angel, nor shall I meet again with thee till thou hast undergone thy days of trial."

Elijah took the boy by the hand and they began to walk aimlessly. The smoke, till then dispersed by the winds, was now concentrated in the streets, making the air impossible to breathe. "Perhaps it's a dream," he thought. "Perhaps it's a nightmare."

"You lied to my mother," the boy said. "The city is destroyed."

"What does that matter? If she did not see what was happening around her, why not allow her to die in peace?"

"Because she trusted you, and said that she was Akbar."

Elijah cut his foot on one of the broken pieces of glass and pottery strewn on the ground. The pain proved to him that he was not dreaming; everything around him was terribly real. They arrived at the square where—how long ago?—he had met with the people and helped them to resolve their disputes; the sky was gilded by flames from the fires.

"I don't want my mother to be this that I'm looking at," the boy insisted. "You lied to her."

The boy was managing to keep his oath; Elijah had not seen a single tear on his face. "What can I do?" he thought. His foot was bleeding, and he decided to concentrate on the pain, to ward off despair.

He looked at the sword cut the Assyrian had made in his body; it was not as deep as he had imagined. He sat down with the boy at the same spot where he had been bound by his enemies, and saved by a traitor. He noticed that people were no longer running; they were walking slowly from place to place, amidst the smoky, dusty ruins, as if they were the living dead. They seemed like souls abandoned by the heavens and condemned to walk the earth eternally. Nothing made sense.

Some of the people reacted; they still heeded the women's voices and the confused orders from the soldiers who had survived the massacre. But they were few and were not achieving any result.

The high priest had once said that the world was the collective dream of the gods. What if, fundamentally, he was right? Could he now help the gods to awaken from this nightmare and then make them sleep again to dream a gentler dream? When Elijah had nocturnal visions, he always awoke and then slept anew; why should the same not occur with the creators of the Universe?

He stumbled over the dead. None of them was now concerned with having to pay taxes, Assyrian encampments in the valley, religious rituals, or the existence of a wandering prophet who perhaps one day had spoken to them.

"I can't remain here permanently. The legacy that she left me is this boy, and I shall be worthy of it, even if it be the last thing I do on the face of the earth."

With a great effort, he rose, took the boy by the hand, and they began to walk. Some of the people were sacking the shops and tents that had been smashed. For the first time, he attempted to react to what had happened, by asking them not to do that.

But the people pushed him aside, saying, "We're eating the remains of what the governor devoured by himself. Get out of the way."

Elijah did not have the strength to argue; he led the boy out of the city, where they began to walk through the valley. The angels, with their swords of fire, would come no more.

"A full moon."

Far from the dust and smoke, he could see the night illuminated by moonlight. Hours before, when he was attempting to leave the city for Jerusalem, he had been able to find his way without difficulty; the Assyrians had had the same advantage.

The boy stumbled over a body and screamed. It was the high priest; his arms and legs had been cut off, but he was still alive. His eyes were fixed on the heights of the Fifth Mountain.

"As you see," he said in a labored but calm voice, "the Phoenician gods have won the celestial battle." Blood was spurting from his mouth.

"Let me end your suffering," Elijah replied.

"Pain means nothing, compared to the joy of having done my duty."

"Your duty was to destroy a city of righteous men?"

"A city does not die, only its inhabitants and the ideas they bore within themselves. One day, others will come to Akbar, drink its water, and the stone that its founder left behind will be polished and cared for by new priests. Leave me now; my pain will soon be over, while your despair will endure for the rest of your life."

The mutilated body was breathing with difficulty, and Elijah left him. At that moment, a group of people—men, women, and children—came running toward him and encircled him.

"It was you!" they shouted. "You dishonored your homeland and brought a curse upon our city!"

"May the gods bear witness to this! May they know who is to blame!"

The men pushed him and shook him by the shoulders. The boy pulled loose from his hands and disappeared. The others struck him in the face, the chest, the back, but his only thoughts were for the boy; he had not even been able to keep him at his side.

The beating did not last long; perhaps his assailants were themselves weary of so much violence. Elijah fell to the ground.

"Leave this place!" someone said. "You have repaid our love with your hatred!"

The group withdrew. Elijah did not have the strength to rise to his feet. When he recovered from the shame, he had ceased to be the same man. He desired neither to die nor to go on living. He desired nothing: he possessed no love, no hate, no faith.

◆

HE AWOKE to someone touching his face. It was still night, but the moon was no longer in the sky.

"I promised my mother that I'd take care of you," the boy said. "But I don't know what to do."

"Go back to the city. The people there are good, and someone will take you in."

"You're hurt. I need to attend to your arm. Maybe an angel will come and tell me what to do."

"You're ignorant, you know nothing about what's happening!" Elijah shouted. "The angels will come no more because we're common folk, and everyone is weak when faced with suffering. When tragedy occurs, let people fend for themselves!"

He took a deep breath, trying to calm himself; there was no point in arguing further.

"How did you find your way here?"

"I never left."

"Then you saw my shame. You saw that there is nothing left for me to do in Akbar."

"You told me that all life's battles teach us something, even those we lose."

He remembered the walk to the well the morning before. But it seemed as if years had passed since then, and he felt the urge to tell him that those beautiful words meant nothing when one faces suffering; but he decided not to upset the boy.

"How did you escape the fire?"

The boy lowered his head. "I hadn't gone to sleep. I decided to spend the night awake, to see if you and my mother were going to meet in her room. I saw the first soldiers come in."

Elijah rose and began to walk. He was looking for the stone in front of the Fifth Mountain where one afternoon he had watched the sunset with the woman.

"I mustn't go," he thought. "I'll become even more desperate."

But some force drew him in that direction. When he arrived there, he wept bitterly; like the city of Akbar, the spot was marked by a stone, but he alone in that entire valley understood its significance; it would neither be praised by new inhabitants, nor polished by couples discovering the meaning of love.

He took the boy in his arms and once again slept.

"I'M HUNGRY AND THIRSTY," THE BOY TOLD ELIJAH AS soon as he awoke.

"We can go to the home of one of the shepherds who live nearby. It's likely nothing happened to them because they didn't live in Akbar."

"We need to repair the city. My mother said that she was Akbar."

What city? No longer was there a palace, a market, or walls. The city's good people had turned into robbers, and its young soldiers had been massacred. Nor would the angels return, though this was the least among his problems.

"Do you think that last night's destruction, suffering, and deaths have a meaning? Do you think that it's necessary to destroy thousands of lives to teach someone something?"

The boy looked at him in alarm.

"Put from your mind what I just said," Elijah told him. "We're going to look for the shepherd."

"And we're going to rebuild the city," the boy insisted.

Elijah did not reply. He knew he would no longer be able to use his authority with the people, who accused him of having brought misfortune. The governor had taken flight, the commander was dead; soon Sidon and Tyre might fall under foreign domination. Perhaps the woman was right: the gods were always changing, and this time it was the Lord who had gone away.

"When will we go back there?" the boy asked again.

Elijah took him by the shoulders and began shaking him forcefully.

"Look behind you! You're not some blind angel but a boy who intended to spy on his mother's acts. What do you see? Have you noticed the columns of rising smoke? Do you know what that means?"

"You're hurting me! I want to leave here, I want to go away!"

Elijah stopped, disconcerted at himself: he had never acted in such a way. The boy broke loose and began running toward the city. Elijah overtook him and kneeled at his feet.

"Forgive me. I don't know what I'm doing."

The boy sobbed, but not a single tear ran down his cheeks. Elijah sat beside him, waiting for him to regain his calm.

"Don't leave," he asked. "When your mother went away, I promised her I'd stay with you until you could follow your own path."

"You also promised that the city was whole. And she said—"

"There's no need to repeat it. I'm confused, lost in my own guilt. Give me time to find myself. I didn't mean to hurt you."

The boy embraced him. But his eyes shed no tears.

◆

THEY CAME TO THE HOUSE in the middle of the valley; a woman was at the door, and two children were playing in front. The flock was in the enclosure, which meant that the shepherd had not yet left for the mountains that morning.

Startled, the woman looked at the man and boy walking toward her. Her instinct was to send them away at once, but custom—and the gods—demanded that she honor the universal law of hospitality. If she did not receive them now, her own children might in the future suffer the same fate.

"I have no money," she said. "But I can give you a little water and something to eat."

They sat on a small porch with a straw roof, and she brought dried fruit and a jar of water. They ate in silence, experiencing, for the first time since the events of the night before, something of the normal routine that marked their every day. The children, frightened by the newcomers' appearance, had taken refuge inside the house.

When they finished their meal, Elijah asked about the shepherd.

"He'll be here soon," she said. "We heard a lot of noise, and somebody came by this morning saying that Akbar had been destroyed. He went to see what happened."

The children called her, and she went inside.

"It will avail me nothing to try to convince the boy," Elijah thought. "He'll not leave me in peace until I do what he asks. I must show him that it is impossible; only then will he be persuaded."

The food and water achieved a miracle: he again felt himself a part of the world.

His thoughts flowed with incredible speed, seeking solutions rather than answers.

◆

SOME TIME LATER, the aged shepherd arrived. He looked at the man and boy with fear, concerned for the safety of his family. But he quickly understood what was happening.

"You must be refugees from Akbar," he said. "I've just returned from there."

"And what's happening?" asked the boy.

"The city was destroyed, and the governor ran away. The gods have disorganized the world."

"We lost everything we had," said Elijah. "We ask that you receive us."

"I think my wife has already received you, and fed you. Now you must leave and face the unavoidable."

"I don't know what to do with the boy. I'm in need of help."

"Of course you know. He's young, he seems intelligent, and he has energy. And you have the experience of someone who's known many victories and defeats in life. The combination is perfect, because it can help you to find wisdom."

The man looked at the wound on Elijah's arm. He said it was not serious; he entered the house and returned with some herbs and a piece of cloth. The boy helped him apply the poultice. When the shepherd said that he could do it alone, the boy told him that he had promised his mother to take care of this man.

The shepherd laughed.

"Your son is a man of his word."

"I'm not his son. And he's a man of his word too. He'll rebuild the city because he has to bring my mother back, the way he did with me."

Suddenly, Elijah understood the boy's concern, but before he could do anything, the shepherd shouted to his wife, who was coming out of the house at that moment. "It's better to start rebuilding life right away," he said. "It will take a long time for everything to return to what it was."

"It will never return."

"You look like a wise young man, and you can understand many things that I cannot. But nature has taught me something that I shall never forget: a man who depends on the weather and the seasons, as only a shepherd does, manages to survive the unavoidable. He cares for his flock, treats each animal as if it were the only one, tries to help the mothers with their young, is never too far from a place where the animals can drink. Still, now and again one of the lambs to which he gave so much of himself dies in an accident. It might be a snake, some wild animal, or even a fall over a cliff. But the unavoidable always happens."

Elijah looked in the direction of Akbar and recalled his conversation with the angel. The unavoidable always happens.

"You need discipline and patience to overcome it," the shepherd said.

"And hope. When that no longer exists, one can't waste his energy fighting against the impossible."

"It's not a question of hope in the future. It's a question of re-creating your own past."

The shepherd was no longer in a hurry; his heart was filled with pity for the refugees who stood facing him. As he and his family had been spared the tragedy, it cost nothing to help them, and thus to thank the gods. Moreover, he had heard talk of the Israelite prophet who had climbed the Fifth Mountain without being slain by the fire from heaven; everything indicated that it was the man before him.

"You can stay another day if you wish."

"I didn't understand what you said before," commented Elijah. "About re-creating your own past."

"I have long seen people passing through here on their way to Sidon and Tyre. Some of them complained that they had not achieved anything in Akbar and were setting out for a new destiny.

"One day these people would return. They had not found what they were seeking, for they carried with them, along with their bags, the weight of their earlier failure. A few returned with a government position, or with the joy of having given their children a better life, but nothing more. Their past in Akbar had left them fearful, and they lacked the confidence in themselves to take risks.

"On the other hand, there also passed my door people full of ardor. They had profited from every moment of life in Akbar and through great effort had accumulated the money for their journey. To these people, life was a constant triumph and would go on being one.

"These people also returned, but with wonderful tales to tell. They had achieved everything they desired because they were not limited by the frustrations of the past."

◆

THE SHEPHERD'S WORDS touched Elijah's heart.

"It is not difficult to rebuild a life, just as it is not impossible to raise Akbar from its ruins," the shepherd continued. "It is enough to be aware that we go on with the same strength that we had before. And to use that in our favor."

The man gazed into Elijah's eyes.

"If you have a past that dissatisfies you, forget it now," he went on. "Imagine a new story of your life, and believe in it. Concentrate only on those moments in which you achieved what you desired, and this strength will help you to accomplish what you want."

"There was a moment when I desired to be a carpenter, and later I wanted to be a prophet sent to save Israel," Elijah thought. "Angels descended from the heavens, the Lord spoke to me. Until I understood that He is not just and that His motives are always beyond my understanding."

The shepherd called to his wife, saying that he was not leaving; he had already been to Akbar on foot, and he was too weary to walk farther.

"Thank you for receiving us," Elijah said.

"It is no burden to shelter you for one night."

The boy interrupted the conversation. "We want to go back to Akbar."

"Wait till morning. The city is being sacked by its own inhabitants, and there is nowhere to sleep."

The boy looked at the ground, bit his lip, and once again held back tears. The shepherd led them into the house, calmed his wife and children, and, to distract them, spent the rest of the day talking about the weather.

THE NEXT DAY THEY AWOKE EARLY, ATE THE MEAL PRE-
pared by the shepherd's wife, and went to the door of the house.

"May your life be long and your flock grow ever larger," said
Elijah. "I have eaten what my body had need of, and my soul has
learned what it did not know. May God never forget what you
did for us, and may your sons not be strangers in a strange
land."

"I don't know to which God you refer; there are many who
dwell on the Fifth Mountain," the shepherd said brusquely, then
quickly changed his tone. "Remember the good things you have
done. They will give you courage."

"I have done very few such things, and none of them was
because of my abilities."

"Then it's time to do more."

"Perhaps I could have prevented the invasion."

The shepherd laughed.

"Even if you were governor of Akbar, you would not be able to stop the unavoidable."

"Perhaps the governor of Akbar should have attacked the Assyrians when they first arrived in the valley with few troops. Or negotiated peace, before war broke out."

"Everything that could have happened but did not is carried away with the wind and leaves no trace," said the shepherd. "Life is made of our attitudes. *And there are certain things that the gods oblige us to live through.* Their reason for this does not matter, and there is no action we can take to make them pass us by."

"Why?"

"Ask a certain Israelite prophet who lived in Akbar. He seems to have the answer to everything."

The man went to the fence. "I must take my flock to pasture," he said. "Yesterday they didn't go out, and they're impatient."

He took his leave with a wave of his hand, departing with his sheep.

THE BOY AND THE MAN WALKED THROUGH THE VALLEY.

"You're walking slowly," the boy said. "You're afraid of what might happen to you."

"I'm afraid only of myself," Elijah replied. "They can do me no harm because my heart has ceased to be."

"The God that brought me back from death is alive. He can bring back my mother, if you do the same thing to the city."

"Forget that God. He's far away and no longer does the miracles we hope for from Him."

The old shepherd was right. From this moment on, it was necessary to reconstruct his own past, forget that he had once thought himself to be a prophet who would free Israel but had failed in his mission of saving even one city.

The thought gave him a strange sense of euphoria. For the

first time in his life he felt free, ready to do whatever he desired whenever he wished. True, he would hear no more angels, but as compensation he was free to return to Israel, to go back to work as a carpenter, to travel to Greece to learn the thoughts of wise men, or to journey with Phoenician navigators to the lands across the sea.

First, however, he must avenge himself. He had dedicated the best years of his youth to an unheeding God who was constantly giving commands and always did things in His own fashion. Elijah had learned to accept His decisions and to respect His designs.

But his loyalty had been rewarded by abandonment, his dedication had been ignored, his efforts to comply with the Supreme Being's will had led to the death of the only woman he had ever loved.

"Thou hast the strength of the world and the stars," said Elijah in his native tongue, so that the boy beside him would not understand the words. "Thou canst destroy a city, a country, as we destroy insects. Send, then, Thy fire from heaven and end my life, for if Thou dost not, I shall go against Thy handiwork."

Akbar loomed in the distance. He took the boy's hand and grasped it tightly.

"From this moment until we go through the city gates, I am going to walk with my eyes closed, and you must guide me," he told the boy. "If I die on the way, do what you have asked me to do: rebuild Akbar, even if to do so you must first grow to manhood and learn to cut wood or work stone."

The boy did not reply. Elijah closed his eyes and allowed himself to be led. He heard the blowing of the wind and the sound of his own steps in the sand.

He remembered Moses, who, after liberating the Chosen People and leading them through the desert, surmounting enormous difficulties, had been forbidden by God to enter Canaan. At the time, Moses had said:

"*I pray Thee, let me go over, and see the good land that is beyond Jordan.*"

The Lord, however, had been offended by his entreaty. And He had answered, "*Let it suffice thee; speak no more unto Me of this matter. Lift up thine eyes westward, and northward, and southward, and eastward, and behold it with thine eyes; for thou shalt not go over this Jordan.*"

Thus had the Lord rewarded the long and arduous task of Moses: He had not permitted him to set foot in the Promised Land. What would have happened if he had disobeyed?

Elijah again turned his thoughts to the heavens.

"O Lord, this battle was not between Assyrians and Phoenicians but between Thee and me. Thou didst not foretell to me our singular war, and as ever, Thou hast triumphed and seen Thy will made manifest. Thou hast destroyed the woman I loved and the city that took me in when I was far from my homeland."

The sound of the wind was louder in his ears. Elijah was afraid, but he continued.

"I cannot bring the woman back, but I can change the fate of Thy work of destruction. Moses accepted Thy will and did not cross the river. But I shall go forward: slay me now, because if Thou allowest me to arrive at the gates of the city, I shall rebuild that which Thou wouldst sweep from the face of the earth. And I shall go against Thy judgment."

He fell silent. He emptied his mind and waited for death. For a long time he concentrated on nothing beyond the sound of his footsteps in the sand; he did not want to hear the voices of angels or threats from heaven. His heart was free, and no longer did he fear what might befall him. Yet in the depths of his soul was the beginning of disquiet, as if he had forgotten a thing of importance.

After much time had passed, the boy stopped, then tugged on Elijah's arm.

"We've arrived," he said.

Elijah opened his eyes. The fire from heaven had not descended on him, and before him were the ruined walls of Akbar.

HE LOOKED AT THE BOY, WHO NOW CLUTCHED ELIJAH'S hand as if fearing that he might escape. Did he love him? He had no idea. But such reflections could wait till later; for now, he had a task to carry out—the first in many years not imposed upon him by God.

From where they stood, he could smell the odor of burning. Scavenger birds circled overhead, awaiting the right moment to devour the corpses of the sentinels that lay rotting in the sun. Elijah approached one of the fallen soldiers and took the sword from his belt. In the confusion of the previous night, the Assyrians had forgotten to gather up the weapons outside the city walls.

"Why do you want that?" the boy asked.

"To defend myself."

"The Assyrians aren't here anymore."

"Even so, it's good to have it with me. We have to be prepared."

His voice shook. It was impossible to know what might happen from the moment they crossed the half-destroyed wall, but he was ready to kill whoever tried to humiliate him.

"Like this city, I too was destroyed," he told the boy. "But also like this city, I have not yet completed my mission."

The boy smiled.

"You're talking the way you used to," he said.

"Don't be fooled by words. Before, I had the objective of removing Jezebel from the throne and turning Israel back to the Lord; now that He has forgotten us, we must forget Him. My mission is to do what you have asked of me."

The boy looked at him warily.

"Without God, my mother will not come back from the dead."

Elijah ran his hand over the boy's hair.

"Only your mother's body has gone away. She is still among us, and as she told us, she is Akbar. We must help her recover her beauty."

◆

THE CITY was almost deserted. Old people, women, and children were walking aimlessly through its streets, in a repetition of the scene he had witnessed the night of the invasion. They seemed uncertain of what to do next.

Each time Elijah's path crossed that of someone else, the boy saw him grip the handle of his sword. But the people displayed indifference; most recognized the prophet from Israel, some nodded at him, but none directed a single word to him, not even one of hatred.

"They've lost even the sense of rage," he thought, looking toward the top of the Fifth Mountain, the summit of which was covered as always by its eternal clouds. Then he recalled the Lord's words:

"I will cast your carcasses upon the carcasses of your idols, and my soul shall abhor you. And I will make your cities waste, and bring the land into desolation.

"And upon them that are left alive of you I will send a faintness into their hearts; and the sound of a shaken leaf shall chase them; and they shall fall when none pursueth."

"Behold, O Lord, what Thou hast wrought: Thou hast kept Thy promise, and the living dead still walk the earth. And Akbar is the city chosen to shelter them."

Elijah and the boy continued to the main square, where they sat and rested on pieces of rubble while they surveyed their surroundings. The destruction seemed more severe and unrelenting than he had thought; the roofs of most of the houses had collapsed; filth and insects had taken over everything.

"The dead must be removed," he said. "Or plague will enter the city through the main gate."

The boy kept his eyes downward.

"Raise your head," Elijah said. "We have much work to do, so your mother can be content."

But the boy did not obey; he was beginning to understand: somewhere among the ruins was the body that had brought him into life, and that body was in a condition similar to all the others scattered on every side.

Elijah did not insist. He rose, lifted a corpse to his shoulders, and carried it to the middle of the square. He could not remember the Lord's recommendations about burying the dead; what he must do was prevent the coming of plague, and the only solution was to burn them.

He worked the entire morning. The boy did not stir from his place, nor did he raise his eyes for an instant, but he kept his promise to his mother: no tear dropped to Akbar's soil.

A woman stopped and stood for a time observing Elijah's efforts.

"The man who solved the problems of the living now puts in order the bodies of the dead," she commented.

"Where are the men of Akbar?" Elijah asked.

"They left, and they took with them the little that remained. There is nothing left worth staying for. The only ones who haven't deserted the city are those incapable of leaving: the old, widows, and orphans."

"But they were here for generations. They can't give up so easily."

"Try to explain that to someone who has lost everything."

"Help me," said Elijah, taking another corpse onto his shoulders and placing it on the pile. "We're going to burn them, so that the plague god will not come to visit us. He is horrified by the smell of burning flesh."

"Let the plague god come," said the woman. "And may he take us all, as soon as possible."

Elijah went on with his task. The woman sat down beside the boy and watched what he was doing. After a time, she approached him again.

"Why do you want to save this wretched city?"

"If I stop to reflect on it, I'll conclude I'm incapable of accomplishing what I desire," he answered.

The old shepherd was right: the only solution was to forget a past of uncertainty and create a new history for oneself. The former prophet had died together with a woman in the flames of her house; now he was a man without faith in God and beset by doubts. But he was still alive, even after challenging divine retribution. If he wished to continue on this path, he must do what he had proposed.

The woman chose one of the lighter bodies and dragged it by the heels, taking it to the pile that Elijah had started.

"It's not from fear of the plague god," she said. "Or for Akbar, since the Assyrians will soon return. It's for that boy sitting there with his head hanging; he has to learn that he still has his life ahead of him."

"Thank you," said Elijah.

"Don't thank me. Somewhere in these ruins we'll find the body of my son. He was about the same age as the boy."

She lifted her hand to her face and wept copiously. Elijah took her gently by the arm.

"The pain you and I feel will never go away, but work will help us to bear it. Suffering has no strength to wound a weary body."

They spent the entire day at the macabre task of collecting and piling up the dead; most of them were youths, whom the Assyrians had identified as part of Akbar's army. More than once he recognized friends, and wept—but he did not interrupt his task.

◆

AT THE END of the afternoon, they were exhausted. Even so, the work done was far from sufficient, and no other inhabitant of Akbar had assisted.

The pair approached the boy, who lifted his head for the first time.

"I'm hungry," he said.

"I'm going to go look for something," the woman answered. "There's plenty of food hidden in the various houses in Akbar; people were preparing for a long siege."

"Bring food for me and for yourself, for we are ministering to the city with the sweat of our brows," said Elijah. "But if the boy wants to eat, he will have to take care of himself."

The woman understood; she would have done the same with her son. She went to the place where her house had stood; almost everything had been ransacked by looters in search of objects of value, and her collection of vases, created by the great master glassmakers of Akbar, lay in pieces on the floor. But she found the dried fruits and grain that she had cached.

She returned to the square, where she divided part of the food with Elijah. The boy said nothing.

An old man approached them.

"I saw that you spent all day gathering the bodies," he said. "You're wasting your time; don't you know the Assyrians will be back, after they conquer Sidon and Tyre? Let the plague god come here and destroy them."

"We're not doing this for them, or for ourselves," Elijah answered. "She is working to teach a child that there is still a future. And I am working to show him there is no longer a past."

"So the prophet is no more a threat to the great princess of Sidon: what a surprise! Jezebel will rule Israel till the end of her days, and we shall always have a refuge if the Assyrians are not generous to the conquered."

Elijah did not reply. The name that had once awakened in him such hatred now sounded strangely distant.

"Akbar will be rebuilt, in any case," the old man insisted. "The gods choose where cities are erected, and they will not abandon it; but we can leave that labor for the generations to come."

"We can, but we will not."

Elijah turned his back on the old man, ending the conversation.

The three of them slept in the open air. The woman embraced the boy, noting that his stomach was growling from hunger. She considered giving him food but quickly dismissed the idea: fatigue truly did diminish pain, and the boy, who seemed to be suffering greatly, needed to busy himself with something. Perhaps hunger would persuade him to work.

THE NEXT DAY, ELIJAH AND THE WOMAN RESUMED their labors. The old man who had approached them the night before came to them again.

"I don't have anything to do and I could help you," he said. "But I'm too weak to carry bodies."

"Then gather bricks and small pieces of wood. Sweep away the ashes."

The old man began doing as they asked.

WHEN THE SUN reached its zenith, Elijah sat on the ground, exhausted. He knew that his angel was at his side, but he could not hear him. "To what avail? He was unable to help me when I needed him, and now I don't want his counsel; all I desire is to put this city in order, to show God I can face Him, and then leave for wherever I want to go."

Jerusalem was not far away, just seven days' travel on foot, with no really difficult places to pass through, but there he was hunted as a traitor. Perhaps it would be better to go to Damascus, or find work as a scribe in some Greek city.

He felt something touch him. He turned and saw the boy holding a small jar.

"I found it in one of the houses," the boy said.

It was full of water. Elijah drank it to the final drop.

"Eat something," he said. "You're working and deserve your reward."

For the first time since the night of the invasion, a smile appeared on the boy's lips, and he ran to the spot where the woman had left the fruits and grain.

Elijah returned to his work, entering destroyed homes, pushing aside the rubble, picking up the bodies, and carrying them to the pile in the middle of the square. The bandage that the shepherd had put on his arm had fallen off, but that mattered little; he had to prove to himself that he was strong enough to regain his dignity.

The old man, who now was amassing the refuse scattered throughout the square, was right: soon the enemy would be back, to harvest fruits they had not sown. Elijah was laboring for the invaders—the assassins of the only woman he had ever loved in his life. The Assyrians were superstitious and would rebuild

Akbar in any case. According to ancient beliefs, the gods had spaced the cities in an organized manner, in harmony with the valleys, the animals, the rivers, the seas. In each of these they had set aside a sacred place to rest during their long voyages about the world. When a city was destroyed, there was always a great risk that the skies would tumble to the earth.

Legend said that the founder of Akbar had passed through there, hundreds of years before, journeying from the north. He decided to sleep at the spot and, to mark where he had left his things, planted a wooden staff upright in the ground. The next day, he was unable to withdraw it, and he quickly understood the will of the Universe; he marked with a stone the place where the miracle had occurred, and he discovered a spring nearby. Little by little, tribes began settling around the stone and the well; Akbar was born.

The governor had once explained to Elijah that, following Phoenician custom, every city was the *third point*, the element linking the will of heaven to the will of the earth. The Universe made the seed transform itself into a plant, the soil allowed it to grow, man harvested it and took it to the city, where the offerings to the gods were consecrated before they were left at the sacred mountains. Even though he had not traveled widely, Elijah was aware that a similar vision was shared by many nations of the world.

The Assyrians feared leaving the gods of the Fifth Mountain without food; they had no desire to disturb the equilibrium of the Universe.

"Why am I thinking such thoughts, if this is a struggle between my will and that of the Lord, who has left me alone in the midst of tribulations?"

The sensation he had felt the day before, when he challenged God, returned: he was forgetting something of importance, and however much he forced his memory, he could not recall it.

ANOTHER DAY WENT BY. MOST OF THE BODIES HAD
been collected when a second woman approached.

"I have nothing to eat," she said.

"Nor have we," answered Elijah. "Yesterday and today we
divided among three what had been intended for one. Discover
where you can obtain food, then inform me."

"Where can I learn that?"

"Ask the children. They know everything."

Ever since he had offered Elijah water, the boy had seemed
to recover some part of his taste for life. Elijah had told him to
help the old man gather up the trash and debris but had not succeeded in keeping him working for long; he was now playing
with the other boys in a corner of the square.

"It's better this way. He'll have his time to sweat when he's a man." But Elijah did not regret having made him spend an entire night hungry, under the pretext that he must work; if he had treated him as a poor orphan, the victim of the evil of murderous warriors, he would never have emerged from the depression into which he had been plunged when they entered the city. Now Elijah planned to leave him by himself for a few days to find his own answers to what had taken place.

"How can children know anything?" said the woman who had asked him for food.

"See for yourself."

The woman and the old man who were helping Elijah saw her talking to the young boys playing in the street. They said something, and she turned, smiled, and disappeared around one corner of the square.

"How did you find out that the children knew?" the old man asked.

"Because I was once a boy, and I know that children have no past," he said, remembering once again his conversation with the shepherd. "They were horrified the night of the invasion, but they're no longer concerned about it; the city has been transformed into an immense park where they can come and go without being bothered. Naturally they would come across the food that people had put aside to withstand the siege of Akbar.

"A child can always teach an adult three things: to be happy for no reason, to always be busy with something, and to know how to demand with all his might that which he desires. It was because of that boy that I returned to Akbar."

◆

THAT AFTERNOON, more old men and women added their numbers to the labor of collecting the dead. The children put to flight the scavenger birds and brought pieces of wood and cloth. When night fell, Elijah set fire to the immense pile of corpses. The survivors of Akbar contemplated silently the smoke rising to the heavens.

As soon as the task was completed, Elijah was felled by exhaustion. Before sleeping, however, the sensation he had felt that morning came again: something of importance was struggling desperately to enter his memory. It was nothing that he had learned during his time in Akbar but an ancient story, one that seemed to make sense of everything that was happening.

◆

THAT NIGHT, a man entered Jacob's tent and wrestled with him until the break of day. And when he saw that he prevailed not against him, he said, "Let me go."

Jacob answered, "I will not let thee go, except thou bless me."

Then the man said to him: "As a prince, hast thou power with God and with men, and hast prevailed. What is thy name?" And he said, Jacob.

And the man answered: "Thy name shall be called no more Jacob, but Israel."

ELIJAH AWOKE WITH A START AND LOOKED AT THE FIRMA-
ment. That was the story that was missing!

Long ago, the patriarch Jacob had encamped, and during the
night, someone had entered his tent and wrestled with him until
daybreak. Jacob accepted the combat, even knowing that his
adversary was the Lord. At morning, he had still not been
defeated; and the combat ceased only when God agreed to bless
him.

The story had been transmitted from generation to generation so that no one would ever forget: *sometimes it was necessary to
struggle with God.* Every human being at some time had tragedy
enter his life; it might be the destruction of a city, the death of a
son, an unproved accusation, a sickness that left one lame forever.
At that moment, God challenged one to confront Him and to

answer His question: "Why dost thou cling fast to an existence so short and so filled with suffering? What is the meaning of thy struggle?"

The man who did not know how to answer this question would resign himself, while another, one who sought a meaning to existence, feeling that God had been unjust, would challenge his own destiny. It was at this moment that fire of a different type descended from the heavens—not the fire that kills but the kind that tears down ancient walls and imparts to each human being his true possibilities. Cowards never allow their hearts to blaze with this fire; all they desire is for the changed situation to quickly return to what it was before, so they can go on living their lives and thinking in their customary way. The brave, however, set afire that which was old and, even at the cost of great internal suffering, abandon everything, including God, and continue onward.

"The brave are always stubborn."

From heaven, God smiles contentedly, for it was this that He desired, that each person take into his hands the responsibility for his own life. For, in the final analysis, He had given His children the greatest of all gifts: the capacity to choose and determine their acts.

Only those men and women with the sacred flame in their hearts had the courage to confront Him. And they alone knew the path back to His love, for they understood that tragedy was not punishment but challenge.

Elijah retraced in his mind each of his steps. Upon leaving the carpentry shop, he had accepted his mission without dispute. Even though it was real—and he felt it was—he had never had the opportunity to see what was happening in the paths that he had chosen not to follow because he feared losing his faith, his dedication, his will. He thought it very dangerous to experience the path of common folk—he might become accustomed to it and find pleasure in what he saw. He did not understand that he was a person like any other, even if he heard angels and now and again received orders from God; in his certainty that he knew what he wanted, he had acted in the selfsame way as those who at no time in their lives had ever made an important decision.

He had fled from doubt. From defeat. From moments of indecision. But the Lord was generous and had led him to the abyss of the unavoidable, to show him that man must *choose*—and not *accept*—his fate.

Many, many years before, on a night like this, Jacob had not allowed God to leave without blessing him. It was then that the Lord had asked: "*What is thy name?*"

The essential point was this: to have a name. When Jacob had answered, God had baptized him *Israel*. Each one has a name from birth but must learn to baptize his life with the word he has chosen to give meaning to that life.

"I am *Akbar*," she had said.

The destruction of the city and the death of the woman he

loved had been necessary for Elijah to understand that he too must have a name. And at that moment he named his life *Liberation*.

◆

HE STOOD and looked at the square before him: smoke still rose from the ashes of those who had lost their lives. By setting fire to the bodies he had challenged an ancient custom of the country, which demanded that the dead be buried in accord with ritual. He had struggled with God and with custom by choosing incineration, but he felt no sense of sin when a new solution was needed to a new problem. God was infinite in His mercy, and implacable in His severity with those who lacked the courage to dare.

He looked around the square again: some of the survivors still had not slept and kept their gaze fixed on the flames, as if the fire were also consuming their memories, their pasts, Akbar's two hundred years of peace and torpor. The time for fear and hope had ended: now there remained only rebuilding or defeat.

Like Elijah, they too could choose a name for themselves. *Reconciliation, Wisdom, Lover, Pilgrim*—there were as many choices as stars in the sky, but each one had need to give a name to his life.

Elijah rose and prayed, "I fought Thee, Lord, and I am not ashamed. And because of it I discovered that I am on my path because such is my wish, not because it was imposed on me by my father and mother, by the customs of my country, or even by Thee.

"It is to Thee, O Lord, that I would return at this moment. I wish to praise Thee with the strength of my will and not with the cowardice of one who has not known how to choose another path. But for Thee to confide to me Thy important mission, I must continue this battle against Thee, until Thou bless me."

To rebuild Akbar. What Elijah thought was a challenge to God was, in truth, his reencounter with Him.

THE WOMAN WHO HAD ASKED ABOUT FOOD REAP-
peared the next morning. She was accompanied by several other
women.

"We found some deposits," she said. "Because so many died,
and so many fled with the governor, we have enough food for a
year."

"Seek older people to oversee the distribution of food,"
Elijah said. "They have experience at organization."

"The old ones have lost the will to live."

"Ask them to come anyway."

The woman was making ready to leave when Elijah stopped
her.

"Do you know how to write, using letters?"

"No."

"I have learned, and I can teach you. You'll need this skill to help me administer the city."

"But the Assyrians will return."

"When they arrive, they'll need our help to manage the affairs of the city."

"Why should we do this for the enemy?"

"So that each of us can give a name to his life. The enemy is only a pretext to test our strength."

◆

AS ELIJAH HAD FORESEEN, the old people came.

"Akbar needs your help," he told them. "Because of that, you don't have the luxury of being old; we need the youth that you once had and have lost."

"We do not know where to find it," one of them replied. "It vanished among the wrinkles and the disillusion."

"That's not true. You never had illusions, and it is that which caused your youth to hide itself away. Now is the moment to find it again, for we have a dream in common: to rebuild Akbar."

"How can we do the impossible?"

"With ardor."

Eyes veiled behind sorrow and discouragement made an effort to shine again. They were no longer the useless citizens who attended judgments searching for something to talk about later in the day; now they had an important mission before them. They were needed.

The stronger among them separated the usable materials from the damaged houses and utilized them to repair those that were still standing. The older ones helped spread in the fields the ashes of the incinerated bodies, so that the city's dead might be remembered at the next harvest; others took on the task of separating the grains stocked haphazardly throughout the city, making bread, and raising water from the well.

Two nights later, Elijah gathered all the inhabitants in the square, now cleared of most of the debris. Torches
were lit, and he began to speak.

"We have no choice," he said. "We can leave this work for
the foreigner to do; but that means giving away the only chance
that a tragedy offers us: that of rebuilding our lives.

"The ashes of the dead that we burned some days ago will
become the plants that are reborn in the spring. The son who was
lost the night of the invasion will become the many children running freely through the ruined streets and amusing themselves by
invading forbidden places and houses they had never known.
Until now only the children have been able to overcome what took
place, because they have no past—for them, everything that matters is the present moment. So we shall try to act as they do."

"Can a man cast from his heart the pain of a loss?" asked a woman.

"No. But he can find joy in something won."

Elijah turned, pointed to the top of the Fifth Mountain, forever covered in clouds. The destruction of the walls had made it visible from the middle of the square.

"I believe in One God, though you think that the gods dwell in those clouds on the Fifth Mountain. I don't want to argue whether my God is stronger or more powerful; I would speak not of our differences but of our similarities. Tragedy has united us in a single sentiment: despair. Why has that come to pass? Because we thought that everything was answered and decided in our souls, and we could accept no changes.

"Both you and I belong to trading nations, but we also know how to act as warriors," he continued. "And a warrior is always aware of what is worth fighting for. He does not go into combat over things that do not concern him, and he never wastes his time over provocations.

"A warrior accepts defeat. He does not treat it as a matter of indifference, nor does he attempt to transform it into a victory. The pain of defeat is bitter to him; he suffers at indifference and becomes desperate with loneliness. After all this has passed, he licks his wounds and begins everything anew. A warrior knows that war is made of many battles; he goes on.

"Tragedies do happen. We can discover the reason, blame others, imagine how different our lives would be had they not occurred. But none of that is important: they did occur, and so be it. From there onward we must put aside the fear that they awoke in us and begin to rebuild.

"Each of you will give yourselves a new name, beginning at this very moment. This will be the sacred name that brings together in a single word all that you have dreamed of fighting for. For my name, I have chosen *Liberation*."

The square was silent for some time. Then the woman who had been the first to help Elijah rose to her feet.

"My name is *Reencounter*," she said.

"My name is *Wisdom*," said an old man.

The son of the widow whom Elijah had loved shouted, "My name is *Alphabet*."

The people in the square burst into laughter. The boy, embarrassed, sat down again.

"How can anybody call himself *Alphabet*?" shouted another boy.

Elijah could have interfered, but it was good for the boy to learn to defend himself.

"Because that was what my mother did," the boy said. "Whenever I look at drawn letters, I'll remember her."

This time no one laughed. One by one, the orphans, widows, and old people of Akbar spoke their names, and their new identities. When the ceremony was over, Elijah asked everyone to go to sleep early: they had to resume their labors the next morning.

He took the boy by the hand, and the two went to the place in the square where a few pieces of cloth had been extended to form a tent.

Starting that night, he began teaching him the writing of Byblos.

THE DAYS BECAME WEEKS, AND THE FACE OF AKBAR was changing. The boy quickly learned to draw the letters and had already begun creating words that made sense; Elijah charged him with writing on clay tablets the history of the rebuilding of the city.

The clay tablets were baked in an improvised oven, transformed into ceramics, and carefully stored away by an aged couple. At the meetings at the end of each afternoon, Elijah asked the old folk to tell of what they had seen in their childhood, and he wrote down the greatest possible number of stories.

"We shall keep Akbar's memory on a material that fire cannot destroy," he explained. "One day our children and the children of their children will know that defeat was not accepted, and that the unavoidable was overcome. This can serve as an example for them."

Each night, after his lessons with the boy, Elijah would walk through the deserted city until he came to the beginning of the road leading to Jerusalem; he would think about departing, then turn around.

The heavy work demanded that he concentrate on the present moment. He knew that the inhabitants of Akbar were relying on him for the rebuilding; he had already disappointed them once, when he had been unable to prevent the death of the enemy general—and thus avoid war. But God always gives His children a second chance, and he must take advantage of this new opportunity. In addition, he was becoming ever fonder of the boy and desired to teach him not only the characters of Byblos but also faith in the Lord and the wisdom of his ancestors.

Even so, he did not forget that in his own land reigned a foreign princess and a foreign god. There were no more angels bearing flaming swords; he was free to leave whenever he desired, and to do whatever he wished.

Each night, he thought of departing. And each night he would lift his hands to the heavens and pray.

"Jacob fought the whole night through and was blessed at daybreak. I have fought Thee for days, for months, and Thou refusest me Thy ear. But if Thou lookest about Thee, Thou wilt know that I am winning: Akbar is rising from its ruins, and I am rebuilding what Thou, using the Assyrian sword, made ashes and dust.

"I shall struggle with Thee until Thou bless me, and bless the fruits of my labor. One day Thou shalt have to answer me."

◆

WOMEN AND CHILDREN carried water to the fields, struggling against the drought that seemed to have no end. One day, when the inclement sun shone down in all its force, Elijah heard someone say, "We work without ceasing, we no longer recall the pains of that night, and we even forget that the Assyrians will return as soon as they have sacked Tyre, Sidon, Byblos, and all of Phoenicia. This is a good thing for us.

"But because we concentrate so much on rebuilding the city, it seems that everything remains the same; we do not see the result of our effort."

Elijah reflected for some time on what he had heard. And he ordered that, at the end of each day of work, the people gather at the foot of the Fifth Mountain to contemplate together the sunset.

Most were so weary that they exchanged not a word, but they discovered that it is important to allow thought to wander as aimlessly as the clouds in the sky. In this way, anxiety fled from each person's heart and they found inspiration and strength for the day to come.

ELIJAH AWOKE SAYING THAT TODAY HE WOULD NOT LABOR.

"In my land, this is the Day of Atonement."

"There is no sin in your soul," a woman told him. "You have done the best that you can."

"But custom must be maintained. And I shall keep it."

The women left, bearing water for the fields, the old men went back to their task of erecting walls and shaping the wood for doors and windows. The children helped to mold the small clay bricks that would later be baked in fire. Elijah watched them with immense joy in his heart. Then he went out from Akbar and walked toward the valley.

He wandered about aimlessly, praying the prayers that he had learned in childhood. The sun was not yet completely risen, and from the place where he stood he could see the enormous shadow of the Fifth Mountain covering part of the valley. He felt a horrible premonition: the struggle between the God of Israel and the gods of the Phoenicians would go on for many generations, and for many thousands of years.

◆

HE RECALLED that one night he had climbed to the top of the mountain and spoken with an angel. But since Akbar's destruction he had never again heard the voices from heaven.

"O Lord, today is the Day of Atonement, and my list of sins against Thee is long," he said, turning toward Jerusalem. "I have been weak, for I have forgotten my strength. I have been compassionate when I should have been firm. I have failed to choose, for fear of making the wrong decision. I have yielded before the time to do so, and I have blasphemed when I should have given thanks.

"Still, Lord, I have also a long list of Thy sins against me. Thou hast made me suffer more than was just, by taking from this world one that I loved. Thou hast destroyed the city that received me, Thou hast confounded my search, Thy harshness almost made me forget the love I have for Thee. For all that time I have struggled with Thee, yet Thou dost not accept the worthiness of my combat.

"If we compare the list of my sins with the list of Thy sins, Thou shalt see that Thou art in my debt. But, as today is the Day of Atonement, give me Thy forgiveness and I shall forgive Thee, so that we may go on walking at each other's side."

At that moment, a wind blew, and he heard his angel say to

him, "Thou hast done well, Elijah. God hath accepted thy combat."

Tears streamed from his eyes. He knelt and kissed the valley's arid soil.

"Thanks unto you for having come, for I still have one doubt: is it not a sin to do this?"

The angel said, "If a warrior fight with his instructor, doth he offend him?"

"No. It is the only way to teach the technique that he must learn."

"Then continue, until the Lord call thee back to Israel," said the angel. "Rise and go on proving that thy struggle hath meaning, because thou hast known how to cross the current of the unavoidable. Many navigate it and founder; others are swept to places for which they were not fated. But thou confrontest the crossing with dignity; thou hast guided the path of thy vessel well and transformed pain into action."

"How sad that you are blind," said Elijah. "Otherwise you would see how orphans, widows, old people have been able to rebuild a city. Soon, all will be as it was."

"Would that it not be so," said the angel. "Remember that they have paid a high price so that their lives could be changed."

Elijah smiled. The angel was right.

"Would that thou mightest act as do men who are given a second chance: do not twice commit the same error. Never forget the reason for thy life."

"I shall not forget," he replied, happy that the angel had returned.

CARAVANS NO LONGER CAME THROUGH THE VALLEY; the Assyrians must have destroyed the roads and changed the trade routes. Day after day, children scaled the only turret in the wall that had escaped destruction; they were charged with watching the horizon and alerting the city to the return of enemy warriors. Elijah planned to receive them with dignity and hand over command.

Then he could depart.

But with each passing day the feeling grew that Akbar had become part of his life. Perhaps his mission was not to remove Jezebel from the throne but to be there with these people for the rest of his life, carrying out the humble role of servant for the Assyrian conqueror. He would help to reestablish trade routes, learn the language of the enemy, and during his moments of repose, oversee the library, which was daily more complete.

Whereas on a night already lost in time the city had appeared to be at its end, it now seemed possible to make it even more beautiful than it had been. The work of rebuilding encompassed widening streets, erecting sturdier roofs, and creating an ingenious system for bringing water from the well to the most distant places. And his soul too was being restored; each day he learned something new from the old people, from the children, from the women. That group, which had not abandoned Akbar only because of the absolute impossibility of doing so, was now a competent, disciplined company.

"If the governor had known that they were of such help, he would have created another type of defense, and Akbar would not have been destroyed."

Elijah thought a moment, then saw that he was mistaken. Akbar needed to be destroyed so that all could awaken the forces that lay dormant inside their own being.

Months went by without the Assyrians showing any sign of life. By now Akbar was almost complete, and Elijah could think of the future. The women had repaired pieces of cloth and made new garments from them. The old folk were reorganizing the dwellings and attending to the city's sanitation. The children were helping when asked, but they usually spent the day at play: that is a child's foremost obligation.

Elijah lived with the boy in a small stone house rebuilt on

the site that had once been a storage place for merchandise. Each night the inhabitants of Akbar would sit around a fire in the main square, telling stories that they had heard earlier in their lives, alongside the boy, who noted everything on clay tablets that were baked the next day. The library was growing before their very eyes.

The woman who had lost her son was also learning the characters of Byblos. When Elijah saw that she could create words and phrases, he charged her with teaching the alphabet to the rest of the population; in this way, when the Assyrians returned, they could be used as interpreters or teachers.

"This was just what the high priest wanted to prevent," an old man, who had taken the name *Ocean* because he desired to have a soul as great as the sea, said one afternoon. "That the writing of Byblos survive to threaten the gods of the Fifth Mountain."

"Who can prevent the unavoidable?" Elijah replied.

The people of Akbar would toil by day, watch the sunset together, and recount stories during the night.

Elijah was proud of his work. And with each day that passed he grew more impassioned with it.

One of the children charged with keeping the vigil descended in a run.

"I saw dust on the horizon!" he said excitedly. "The enemy is returning!"

Elijah climbed to the turret and saw that the news was correct.

He reckoned that they would be at the gates of Akbar the next day.

That afternoon he told the inhabitants that they should not attend the sunset but gather in the square. When the day's work was over, he stood before the assembled group and saw that they were afraid.

"Today we shall tell no stories of the past, nor speak of Akbar's future," he said. "We shall talk about ourselves."

No one said a word.

"Some time ago, a full moon shone in the sky. That night, what all of us had foreseen, but did not want to accept, came to pass: Akbar was destroyed. When the Assyrian army departed, the best among our men were dead. Those who had escaped saw that it was futile to remain here, and they determined to go. Only the old, the widows, and the orphans were left—that is, the useless.

"Look about you; the square is more beautiful than ever, the buildings are more solid, the food is divided among us, and everyone is learning the writing invented in Byblos. Somewhere in this city is a collection of tablets on which we have written our stories, and generations yet to be born will remember what we did.

"Today we know that the old, the widows, the orphans, also departed. They left in their place a band of youths of every age, filled with enthusiasm, who have given name and meaning to their lives.

"At each moment of rebuilding, we knew that the Assyrians

would return. We knew that one day we would be obliged to hand our city over to them and, together with the city, our efforts, our sweat, our joy at seeing it more beautiful than before."

The light from the fire illuminated tears coursing down the faces of some of the people. Even the children, who customarily played during the evening meetings, were listening attentively to his words. Elijah continued.

"This does not matter. We have carried out our duty to the Lord because we accepted His challenge and the honor of His struggle. Before that night, He had urged us, saying, *Walk!* But we heeded Him not. Why?

"Because each of us had already decided his own future: I thought only of removing Jezebel from the throne, the woman who is now called *Reencounter* wanted her son to become a navigator, the man who today bears the name *Wisdom* wished merely to spend the rest of his days drinking wine in the square. We were accustomed to the sacred mystery of life and gave little importance to it.

"Then the Lord thought to Himself: *They would not walk? Then let them be idle for a long time!*

"And only then did we understand His message. The steel of Assyrian blades swept away our youth, and cowardice swept away our adults. Wherever they are at this moment, they are still idle; they have accepted God's curse.

"We, however, struggle with the Lord, just as we struggle

with the men and women we love in our lifetimes. For it is that struggle with the divine that blesses us and makes us grow. We grasp the opportunity in the tragedy and do our duty by Him, by proving we were able to obey the order to *walk*. Even in the worst of circumstances, we have forged ahead.

"There are moments when God demands obedience. But there are moments in which He wishes to test our will and challenges us to understand His love. We understood that will when Akbar's walls tumbled to the ground: they opened our horizon and allowed each of us to see his capabilities. We stopped thinking about life and chose to live it.

"The result is good."

Elijah saw that the people's eyes were shining again. They had understood.

"Tomorrow I shall deliver Akbar without a struggle; I am free to leave whenever I choose, for I have done what the Lord expected of me. But my blood, my sweat, and the only love I have known are in the soil of this city, and I have decided to remain here the rest of my days, to prevent its being destroyed again. Make whatever decision you wish but never forget one thing: all of you are much better than you believed.

"Take advantage of the chance that tragedy has given you; not everyone is capable of doing so."

Elijah rose, ending the meeting. He told the boy that he would return late and said he should go to bed without waiting for his arrival.

◆

HE WENT TO THE TEMPLE, the only place that had escaped the destruction and had not needed rebuilding, though the statues of the gods had been taken away by the Assyrians. With all respect, he touched the stone that, according to tradition, marked the spot where an ancestor had embedded a staff in the ground and been unable to wrest it free.

He thought how, in his country, places such as this were being erected by Jezebel, and a part of his people bowed down before Baal and his deities. Once again the premonition ran through his soul that the war between the Lord of Israel and the gods of Phoenicia would go on for a long time, beyond anything his imagination could encompass. As in a vision, he saw stars crossing the sun and raining death and destruction on both countries. Men who spoke strange languages rode animals of steel and dueled in the middle of the clouds.

"It is not this that thou shouldst now see, for the time hath not yet come," he heard his angel say. "Look out the window."

Elijah did as he was ordered. Outside, the full moon illuminated the streets and houses of Akbar, and despite the late hour he could hear conversations and laughter from the city's inhabitants. Even facing the Assyrians' return, the people kept the will to live, ready to confront a new stage in their lives.

He saw a form and knew that it was the woman he had

loved, who now returned to walk with pride through her city. He smiled, feeling her touch his face.

"I am proud," she seemed to be saying. "Akbar truly is still beautiful."

He felt the urge to weep, then remembered the boy, who had never shed a tear for his mother. He checked his sobs and thought anew of the most beautiful parts of the story that together they had lived, from the meeting at the city gates, till the moment she had written the word *love* on a clay tablet. Once again he could see her garment, her chair, the fine sculpting of her nose.

"You told me you were Akbar. Well, I have taken care of you, healed your wounds, and now I return you to life. May you be happy among your new companions.

"And I want to tell you something: I too was Akbar and did not know."

He knew that she was smiling.

"Long since, the desert wind wiped away our footprints in the sand. But at every second of my existence, I remember what happened, and you still walk in my dreams and in my reality. Thank you for having crossed my path."

He slept there, in the temple, feeling the woman caressing his hair.

THE CHIEF TRADER SAW A RAGGED GROUP OF PEOPLE IN the middle of the road. Thinking they were robbers, he ordered the caravan to take up arms.

"Who are you?" he asked.

"We are the people of Akbar," replied a bearded man with shining eyes. The leader of the caravan noticed that he spoke with a foreign accent.

"Akbar was destroyed. We have been charged by the governments of Sidon and Tyre to find a well so caravans can cross the valley again. Communication with the rest of the land cannot be interrupted forever."

"Akbar still exists," the man said. "Where are the Assyrians?"

"The entire world knows where they are," laughed the caravan leader. "Making the soil more fertile. And feeding the birds and wild animals for a long time now."

"But they were a powerful army."

"There's no such thing as power or an army, if we find out where they're going to attack. Akbar sent word that they were approaching, and Sidon and Tyre set an ambuscade for them at the end of the valley. Whoever didn't die in battle was sold as slaves by our navigators."

The ragged people cheered and embraced one another, crying and laughing at the same time.

"Who are you people?" insisted the trader. "And who are you?" he asked, pointing to their leader.

"We are the young warriors of Akbar" was the reply.

◆

THE THIRD HARVEST had begun, and Elijah was the governor of Akbar. There had been great resistance at first; the old governor had attempted to return and reoccupy his position, for such did custom dictate. The inhabitants of the city, however, refused to admit him and for days threatened to poison the water in the well. The Phoenician authorities finally yielded to their demands; after all, Akbar's only importance was the water it supplied to travelers, and the government of Israel was in the hands of a princess of Tyre. By conceding the position of governor to an Israelite, the Phoenician rulers could begin to consolidate a stronger commercial alliance.

The news spread throughout the region, carried by the merchant caravans that had begun circulating again. A minority in Israel considered Elijah the worst of traitors, but at the proper moment Jezebel would take on the task of eliminating this resistance, and peace would return to the region. The princess was content, for one of her worst foes had in the end become her greatest ally.

◆

RUMORS OF A NEW Assyrian invasion began to arise, and the walls of Akbar were rebuilt. A new system of defense was developed, with sentinels and outposts spread between Tyre and Akbar; in this way, if one of the cities was besieged, the other could send troops overland while assuring the delivery of food by sea.

The city prospered before one's very eyes: the new Israelite governor had created a rigorous system, based on writing, to control taxes and merchandise. The old folk of Akbar attended to it all, using new techniques for supervision, and patiently resolved the problems that arose.

The women divided their time between tending to the crops and weaving. During the period of isolation, to recover the small amount of cloth that had remained, they had been obliged to create new patterns of embroidery; when the first merchants arrived in the city, they were enchanted by the designs and placed several orders.

The children too had learned the writing of Byblos; Elijah was certain that one day this would be of help to them.

As was always his wont before the harvest, he strolled through the fields that afternoon, giving thanks to the Lord for the countless blessings bestowed upon him for all these years. He saw people with their baskets filled with grain, and around them children at play. He waved to them, and they returned his greeting.

Smiling, he walked toward the stone where, long ago, he had been given a clay tablet with the word *love*. It was his custom to visit that spot every day to watch the sunset and recall each instant that they had spent together.

"AND IT CAME TO PASS AFTER MANY DAYS, THAT THE WORD OF the Lord came to Elijah in the third year, saying, Go, shew thyself unto Ahab; and I will send rain upon the earth."

FROM THE STONE WHERE HE SAT, ELIJAH SAW THE world shudder about him. The sky turned black for an instant, but the sun quickly shone again.

He saw the light. An angel of the Lord was before him.

"What has happened?" asked Elijah, startled. "Has the Lord pardoned Israel?"

"No," answered the angel. "He desireth that thou return to liberate thy people. Thy struggle with Him is ended, and—at this moment—he hath blessed thee. He hath given thee leave to continue His work in that land."

Elijah was astonished.

"But, now, just when my heart has again found peace?"

"Recall the lesson once taught thee," said the angel. "And recall the words the Lord spake unto Moses:

"*And thou shalt remember all the way which the Lord thy God led thee to humble thee, and to prove thee. To know what was in thine heart.*

"*Lest when thou hast eaten and art full, and hast built goodly houses, and dwelt therein, and when thy herds and thy flocks multiply, then thine heart be lifted up, and thou forget the Lord thy God.*"

Elijah turned to the angel. "What about Akbar?" he asked.

"It can live without thee, for thou hast left an heir. It will survive for many years."

The angel of the Lord disappeared.

ELIJAH AND THE BOY ARRIVED AT THE FOOT OF THE
Fifth Mountain. Weeds had grown between the stones of the
altars; since the high priest's death no one had gone there.

"Let's climb it," he said.

"It's forbidden."

"Yes, it's forbidden. But that doesn't mean it's dangerous."

He took him by both hands, and they began climbing
toward the top. They stopped from time to time to gaze at the
valley below; the absence of rain had left its mark throughout the
countryside, and with the exception of the cultivated fields
around Akbar, everything seemed a desert as harsh as those of
Egypt.

"I've heard my friends say the Assyrians are coming back,"
the boy said.

"That could be, but what we have done was worthwhile; it was the way that God chose to teach us."

"I don't know if He bothers much with us," the boy said. "He didn't have to be so severe."

"He must have tried other means before discovering that we were not listening to Him. We were too accustomed to our lives and no longer read His words."

"Where are they written?"

"In the world around us. Merely be attentive to what happens in your life, and you will discover where, every moment of the day, He hides His words and His will. Seek to do as He asks: this alone is the reason you are in the world."

"If I discover it, I'll write it on clay tablets."

"Do so. But write them, above all, in your heart; there they can be neither burned nor destroyed, and you will take them wherever you go."

They walked for some time more. The clouds were now very close.

"I don't want to go there," the boy said, pointing to them.

"They will do you no harm: they're just clouds. Come with me."

He took him by the hands, and they climbed. Little by little, they found themselves entering the fog. The boy clung to him, and although Elijah tried to talk to him now and again, he said not a word. They walked among the naked rocks of the summit.

"Let's go back," asked the boy.

Elijah decided not to insist; the boy had already experienced great difficulties and much fear in his short life. He did as he was asked; they came out from the fog and could once again discern the valley below.

"Someday, look in Akbar's library for what I wrote for you. It's called *The Manual of the Warrior of Light.*"

"Am I a warrior of light?" replied the boy.

"Do you know what my name is?" asked Elijah.

"*Liberation.*"

"Sit here beside me," said Elijah, pointing to a rock. "I cannot forget my name. I must continue with my task, even if at this moment all I desire is to be at your side. That was why Akbar was rebuilt, to teach us that it is necessary to go onward, however difficult it may appear."

"You're going away."

"How do you know?" he asked, surprised.

"I wrote it on a tablet, last night. Something told me; it may have been my mother, or an angel. But I already felt it in my heart."

Elijah caressed the boy's head.

"You have learned to read God's will," he said contentedly. "So there's nothing that I need to explain to you."

"What I read was the sadness in your eyes. It wasn't difficult. Other friends of mine noticed it too."

"This sadness you read in my eyes is part of my story. Only a small part that will last but a few days. Tomorrow, when I depart for Jerusalem, it will not have the strength it had before, and little by little it will disappear. Sadness does not last forever when we walk in the direction of that which we always desired."

"Is it always necessary to leave?"

"It's always necessary to know when a stage of one's life has ended. If you stubbornly cling to it after the need has passed, you lose the joy and meaning of the rest. And you risk being shaken to your senses by God."

"The Lord is stern."

"Only with those He has chosen."

◆

ELIJAH LOOKED AT AKBAR below. Yes, God sometimes could be very stern, but never beyond a person's capacity: the boy was unaware that they were sitting where Elijah had received an angel of the Lord and learned how to bring him back from the dead.

"Are you going to miss me?" Elijah asked.

"You told me that sadness disappears if we press ahead. There's still much to do to leave Akbar as beautiful as my mother deserves. She walks in its streets."

"Come back to this place when you have need of me. And look toward Jerusalem: I shall be there, seeking to give meaning to my name, *Liberation*. Our hearts are linked forever."

"Was that why you brought me to the top of the Fifth Mountain? So I could see Israel?"

"So you could see the valley, the city, the other mountains, the rocks and clouds. The Lord often has his prophets climb mountains to converse with Him. I always wondered why He did that, and now I know the answer: when we are on high, we can see everything else as small.

"Our glory and our sadness lose their importance. Whatever we conquered or lost remains there below. From the heights of the mountain, you see how large the world is, and how wide its horizons."

The boy looked about him. From the top of the Fifth Mountain, he could smell the sea that bathed the beaches of Tyre. And he could hear the desert wind that blew from Egypt.

"Someday I'll govern Akbar," he told Elijah. "I know what's big. But I also know every corner of the city. I know what needs to be changed."

"Then change it. Don't let things remain idle."

"Couldn't God have chosen a better way of showing us all this? There was a time when I thought He was evil."

Elijah said nothing. He recalled a conversation, many years before, with a Levite prophet while the two awaited death at the hands of Jezebel's soldiers.

"Can God be evil?" the boy insisted.

"God is all-powerful," answered Elijah. "He can do anything, and nothing is forbidden to Him, for if it were, there would exist someone more powerful than He, to prevent His doing certain things. In that case, I should prefer to worship and revere that more powerful someone."

He paused for several instants to allow the boy to fathom the meaning of his words. Then he continued.

"Still, because of His infinite power, He chose to do only Good. If we reach the end of our story, we shall see that often Good is disguised as Evil, but it goes on being the Good, and is part of the plan that He created for humanity."

He took the boy by the hand, and together they descended the mountain in silence.

◆

THAT NIGHT, the boy went to sleep in his arms. As soon as day began to break, Elijah carefully removed him from his bosom so he would not awaken him.

He quickly donned the only garment he possessed and departed. On the road, he picked up a piece of wood from the ground and used it as a staff. He planned never to be without it: it was the remembrance of his struggle with God, of the destruction and rebuilding of Akbar.

Without looking back, he continued toward Israel.

FIVE YEARS LATER, ASSYRIA AGAIN INVADED THE COUNTRY, *this time with a more professional army and more competent generals. All Phoenicia fell under the domination of the foreign conqueror except Tyre and Zarephath, which its inhabitants called Akbar.*

The boy became a man, governed the city, and was judged a sage by his contemporaries. He died in the fullness of his years, surrounded by loved ones and saying always that "it was necessary to keep the city beautiful and strong, for his mother still strolled its streets." Because of their joint system of defense, Tyre and Zarephath were not occupied by the Assyrian king Sennacherib until 701 B.C., almost 160 years after the events related in this book.

From that time on, Phoenician cities never recovered their importance and began to suffer a series of invasion——by the Neo-Babylonians, the

Persians, the Macedonians, the Seleucids, and, finally, by Rome. Even so, they continue to exist in our own time because, according to ancient tradition, the Lord never selected at random the places He wished to see inhabited. Tyre, Sidon, and Byblos are still part of Lebanon, which even today remains a battlefield.

ELIJAH RETURNED TO ISRAEL AND CALLED THE PROPHETS together at Mount Carmel. There he asked them to divide into two groups: those who worshiped Baal, and those who believed in the Lord. Following the angel's instructions, he offered a bullock to the first group and asked them to call out to the heavens for their gods to receive it. The Bible says:

"And it came to pass at noon, that Elijah mocked them, and said, Cry aloud: for he is a god; either he is talking, or he is pursuing, or he is in a journey, or peradventure he sleepeth, and must be awaked.

"And they cried aloud, and cut themselves after their manner with knives and lancets, till the blood gushed out upon them.

"And there was neither voice, nor any to answer, nor any that regarded."

Then Elijah took his animal and offered it, following the angel's instructions. At that moment the fire of heaven descended and "consumed the burnt sacrifice, and the wood, and the stones." Minutes later, a heavy rain fell, ending four years of drought.

From that moment, civil war broke out. Elijah ordered the execution of the prophets who had betrayed the Lord, and Jezebel sought him everywhere, to kill him. He fled, however, to the eastern part of the Fifth Mountain, which faced Israel.

The Syrians invaded the country and killed King Ahab, husband of the princess of Tyre, with an accidentally shot arrow that entered an opening in his armor. Jezebel took refuge in her palace and, following several popular revolts and the rise and fall of various governments, was captured. She preferred leaping from a window to giving herself up to the men sent to arrest her.

Elijah remained on the mountain until the end of his days. The Bible says that one afternoon, when he was conversing with Elisha, the prophet he had named as his successor, "there appeared a chariot of fire, and horses of fire, and parted them both asunder; and Elijah went up by a whirlwind into heaven."

Almost eight hundred years later, Jesus bade Peter, James, and John to climb a mountain. The Gospel according to Matthew relates that Jesus "was transfigured before them; and his face did shine as the sun, and his raiment was white as the light. And, behold, there appeared unto them Moses and Elias talking with him."

Jesus asks the apostles not to speak of this vision until the Son of Man be risen from the dead, but they reply that this will happen only when Elijah returns.

Matthew 17:10–13 tells the rest of the story:

Zd his disciples asked him, saying, Why then say the scribes that Elias must first come?

"And Jesus answered and said unto them, Elias truly shall first come, and restore all things. But I say unto you, That Elias is come already, and they knew him not, but have done unto him whatsoever they listed.

"Then the disciples understood that he spake unto them of John the Baptist."

MARIA CONCEIVED WITHOUT SIN, PRAY FOR US WHO
call on Thee. Amen.

About the Translator

CLIFFORD E. LANDERS is professor of political science at Jersey City State College and a premier translator of Latin American fiction. He has translated into English many of Brazil's top writers, including Jorge Amado, Rubem Fonseca, and Chico Buarque. He lives in Montclair, New Jersey.